FALLING UNDER THE MISTLETOE

EVELYN MAE

CHAPTER 1

Do you have a friend who is always drawn to guys who are bad for them?

That's me. I'm that friend.

I'm not sure if I attract jerks or if there's something about me that makes them that way. Either way, I'm over it, especially after this nightmare of a trip.

The small group that gathered around to claim their bags after the flight is diminishing and mine still hasn't appeared. I just want to get home and back to work at Honey's. At the bakery, I always feel confident and in control. It's my happy place. In relationships? I'm a hot mess, and this fiasco confirms it.

I watch a piece of luggage appear from the back and circle around the conveyor belt for the third time. It is a beat up duffle bag, worn and ragged from its travels, and whoever took it on their trip isn't here to claim it. It looks lonely with no other luggage around.

I feel ya, buddy.

I've been through the wringer and this is not how I wanted

to come back from Jamaica. This getaway with Jake was supposed to invigorate me and put me in the right state of mind for the holidays. Christmas is my busiest time of year at Honey's. Normally, I never would have left the bakery before the mad rush began. But Jake convinced me this was the perfect time to go, even while my gut was telling me to stay home. Why do I keep doing this to myself?

What did they say? The definition of insanity is doing the same thing over and over again and expecting a different result?

I must be crazy.

I am zoning out, deep in the trenches of my mind, when I notice a tall, dark-haired man on his cell phone standing a few feet away.

He is at least 6' tall, with a lean, muscular build that fills out his clothes in all the right places. It is freezing here in Connecticut, but even under his black wool peacoat I can see his broad shoulders and thick biceps. He looks a bit rugged, with the exact right amount of five o'clock shadow along his chiseled jaw that always drives me crazy. Scruffy with a bit of polish gets me every time.

Well, hello handsome. If I'm attracted to you, you must be the absolute worst.

I chuckle to myself as I reach for my purse to grab my phone. My bag has finally appeared on the conveyor belt and, as I am waiting for it to come around, I know I have to document this treat for my single friend Jules who will appreciate the eye candy. After what just happened, I've officially sworn off all men, but I'm happy to pass them along to my friends.

I discreetly snap his photo and just as I am tucking my phone back in my purse, I watch Mr. Scruff n' Muscles walk over to the baggage claim, grab my suitcase, and dart off towards the exit.

Oh my goodness... I'm being robbed!

"Hey!" I yell in a panic. "That guy just stole my bag!" I run after him, onlookers staring, stunned.

"Stop! You! Give me back my suitcase! Help! Someone get security!"

I catch up to him just as he turns around to face me, and I'm surprised he doesn't bolt. I don't have any experience with criminals, but since I was expecting him to run, I don't know what to do now that he has stopped and is confronting me. He might be dangerous, so I stay back a few steps.

He looks confused, looking to both sides as if to help me find the culprit.

"Do you need help, ma'am? Did something happen?"

"Don't act like you don't know what's going on! Give me back my suitcase!"

"Excuse me?" He sounds annoyed, like I am a terrier pulling at his pant leg.

"Look, I've had a long day. Just give me back my bag and you can run out of here before security gets here."

He smirks at me, almost looking amused, and looks me up and down, not hiding that he is checking me out.

That I take notice of the thief's smile further confirms I have the worst taste in men of all time. He must be off his rocker to stick around and find this confrontation fun. I step back further.

Stay calm, Callie.

"I didn't take your bag, but if someone did, I can help you look for him. What did the guy look like?"

"Are you for real? I just saw you take it. That's my bag in your hand and you're going to stand here and pretend you don't know what I'm talking about? Do all men think I'm stupid?"

Exasperated, I lunge for my suitcase to grab it from him and he pulls back, giving me a quizzical look.

"You really think this is yours?" He looks around. "Is this a practical joke? Did my brother Will put you up to this?"

"Stop with the act. You know it's mine. Just give it to me or I'll press charges. I'm not in the mood today for this nonsense."

"I don't know what you think happened, but this is my suitcase," he says matter-of-factly.

I stare at him in disbelief. A crowd is starting to form around us as people overhear the commotion.

Based on his expensive looking outfit, he doesn't look like someone who needs to steal. He runs his hand through his thick, dark brown hair and checks his Rolex, as if he has somewhere to be.

I bet he stole that watch.

His blue eyes lock on mine when he catches me looking him over. He raises an eyebrow and his full lips curve into a devilish smile.

Am I seriously checking out the guy who is stealing from me? I should be in therapy.

A few men who were whispering to each other cautiously walk over. "Buddy, just give the lady her bag."

I sigh, grateful people are stepping up to help. To keep things calm, I decide to try a different tactic; I need to stall until security shows up.

"I know things are tough around the holiday season. There's nothing of value in there that you want, I promise."

The men get to either side of Mr. Sexy Thief, as if they are preparing to grab him in case he darts off, and I can see an Andre-the-Giant-sized security guard quickly barreling in our direction. This grabs his attention, and he puts his hands up in a stop motion.

"Woah, guys, there's obviously been a misunderstanding." He turns to me, looking as self-assured as ever. "Ma'am, would you like to look inside my bag? All my clothes are in there, as well as my sales files with my name on it, so it will be clear it's mine."

I start to sweat. This guy is pathological.

"Sure, whatever you say. Just give me the bag." He rolls it in my direction and shakes his head in disbelief.

"Security is here. You can stop the act. You should have just given it to me and ran when you had the chance." I pause, realizing now that this is almost over I am about to get someone arrested right before Christmas. "I won't press charges, ok?"

He laughs and crosses his arms. "That's quite kind of you, ma'am. So generous."

"And stop calling me ma'am!"

He pinches his fingers together and puts them to his lips, signaling that he is locking his lips and throwing away the key. He throws me an arrogant smile and winks.

The nerve of this freaking guy.

The security guard must be over 6'5" and has the build of a linebacker. His expression says he is no-nonsense, and I instantly feel better. I look at his name tag.

Gus.

This beast's name is Gus? Shouldn't he be a Butch or an Axel?

"What seems to be the problem here?"

"Gus, I'm so glad you're here!" I leap over and am about to go in for a hug when he keeps me away with one hand.

Sheez. Somebody's a grumpy Gus.

"This guy stole my bag, but he just gave it back. He didn't have a chance to rifle through it yet, so I'm pretty sure everything is still here. If you can give him a warning or something, I'm fine with that."

I am awfully proud of myself for being so zen about the whole thing.

"That's my bag she's holding. She's convinced it's hers. If you open it, you'll see my files and all my clothes."

"Ma'am? Do you mind if we open it here?"

I roll my eyes and notice the thief is barely holding back a laugh at him calling me ma'am.

"Please do. I just want this over with already."

Gus reaches down and flips the bag on its side. Just as he is about to unzip it, I spot a sticker on top that looks unfamiliar: a logo for a winery.

I have never been to a winery before.

Oh my goodness. That's not my bag.

CHAPTER 2

CALLIE

"Wait!" I say, frantically.

Gus looks at me, confused. "What's wrong?" A realization flashes across his face and he leans in towards me, lowering his voice to a whisper. "Would you like to do this in a more secluded area? If there are *private* things in here, don't worry about it. Women bring stuff like that when they travel all the time. No need to be embarrassed." He inches in a little closer, as if he is sharing a secret.

I turn red. What does he think I have in that bag?

I look back and forth at the suitcase and the man I have accused in front of me. His smile grows large, like the Cheshire Cat, my embarrassing mistake all over my face.

"Ma'am?" Gus pauses, staring at me, concerned.

"Well… I just noticed something on the bag that doesn't look familiar."

He raises one eyebrow and says in a sharp tone, "Are you saying you now think this *isn't* your bag?"

I give him a meek smile. "Well, it looks almost identical, except for that sticker there." I point to the top of the bag that now clearly shows a *D. Montgomery Vineyard* logo.

Gus opens the bag and, sure enough, men's clothes are neatly folded inside and a file folder is lying on top. He opens the folder and looks at the top page.

"Are you Gabe Montgomery?"

"Sure am." He takes his wallet out and hands him his license.

The men who had come to my rescue groan and walk away. A woman giggles behind me, undoubtedly one of the many people in the crowd who realizes I'm an idiot.

I feel my skin grow hot. "I'm so sorry. I don't know what is wrong with me. That looks exactly like my bag."

I turn around and look back towards the baggage claim area. All the passengers who had been waiting for their luggage are now gone and the only bag that remains is the beat up duffle bag. Mine is still missing.

I shake my head and throw my hands up in defeat. "I don't know what happened. Maybe it got lost in transit... regardless, I'm so sorry for accusing you and wasting everyone's time."

"Definitely made my first time visiting Connecticut interesting." This time, he gives me a genuine smile.

How is he not mad? If someone did that to me, I would flip out. I almost wish he would just yell at me already. Something about him being quick to forgive makes me feel even worse.

Grumpy Gus rattles off something about being glad there wasn't a situation and walks away muttering to himself about wasted time.

"Thanks for being so cool about all this." I push my hair behind my ear and start to slowly walk away. "I'm sorry for causing a scene."

"No worries." He trots up alongside me. "So, your bag is still missing then? Do you need help looking for it?"

"No, it's not over there." I turn and nod in the direction of the conveyor belt. "There's only one bag left, and it's not mine."

"What flight were you on? You don't look familiar."

I look at him, amused. "Do you memorize the faces of all the passengers on your flights?"

He laughs, and even his laugh is deep and sexy. "Well, considering there were only about 15 of us on there, yeah." He pauses for a moment, considering, and then adds, "Regardless, a woman like you would be hard to miss."

I feel butterflies at the compliment, but the rush is quickly squashed as soon as I connect the dots. "Wait. Only 15 passengers? My flight was packed. Were you flying in from Jamaica?"

"No, I wish. I'm coming in from California. I had a layover in Atlanta."

"Nooo." I rush over to the monitor and, sure enough, I had been at the wrong baggage claim. I feel my skin flush all over again.

I can't believe this happened.

"Let me guess: you were at the wrong baggage claim?"

This guy just needs to go. I can't stand any more humiliation right now.

"Something like that. Sorry again for the confusion and thanks for being so human about it all. Happy holidays and I hope you enjoy your trip. The rest of Connecticut isn't crazy like me, I promise."

I don't dare wait for a response and hurry off towards the right area, where I find my bag, and curse myself for jumping to conclusions.

I make a quick call to Jules to see if she is here yet. It goes straight to voicemail. I hang up and shoot her a quick text letting her know I landed and will wait just inside the main entrance.

I walk over to the doors and, in the distance, see Gus. I wave at him and point down to my bag excitedly as if to say, "See! I found it!" and he just shakes his head and turns to face the opposite direction.

Tough crowd.

I stare out the window waiting for Jules. I chuckle to myself, thinking about the drama I caused. Although embarrassing, it did boost my mood a bit. I can't seem to get that man out of my mind. He took all of it in stride and his smile is downright lethal.

Gabe Montgomery. Even his name has a nice ring to it. Not to mention his smokin' hot…

Stop it. No more men. Especially gorgeous scruffy ones.

CHAPTER 3

GABE

I watch her jog off, her long, brown hair flowing behind her. She couldn't get away fast enough. I don't blame her; that was quite the scene.

I laugh to myself, picturing her face when she realized I wasn't some thief trying to steal her luggage, her enticing hazel eyes growing wide with shock. Something about that woman has me wanting to learn more, and it isn't just because she is beautiful.

I noticed her standing at the baggage claim when I first got there and she seemed deep in thought, almost sad. Guarded. Even still, if I had been back home in California, I probably would have found an excuse to go over and talk to her. She has the cutest smattering of freckles across her cheeks that looks even more tempting when she's flushed.

Just my type.

I wanted to help and make sure she found her bag, but I could tell she was embarrassed and trying to get away, so I didn't push it.

Walking through the airport, I see that most of the restaurants are closed. The food on the plane was disgusting, so now

I'm starving. I hoped to grab something quick before I call an Uber. In the distance, it looks like there is a pub towards the exit that I can try before I leave.

My phone vibrates. It's a text from Abby, my realtor, letting me know she has three interested parties scheduled to view the building this week. This is great news because I didn't think many people would want a building that is so run down, especially in such a small town. I shoot her a quick message back, thanking her for the update, and let her know I landed and would touch base tomorrow.

I am just about to walk into the pub when I spot the woman again. This time she is standing with her bag, which truly looks identical to mine, and seems flustered on a call. Curious, I stop a few steps behind her and pretend to look down at my phone as she talks.

"Jules, where are you? You were supposed to be here a half hour ago. I know the flight was late because of the snow, so I'm hoping the roads aren't too bad! Call me and let me know either way. It's freezing out there, so I'm going to wait inside and maybe grab a quick bite. If I don't hear from you within the hour, I'll find a taxi. I hope you're ok! Talk to you soon!"

She puts her phone back into her purse, walks over to side of the pub and slides her back down the wall to sit on the floor. She looks utterly defeated.

What harm could it do to help a beautiful woman?

I walk over and say, "That bag sure looks like mine. You think they're related?"

Startled, she looks up and laughs when she sees it's me. It is the first time I've heard her laugh, and I promise myself I will make her do it again. I like the way she looks at me. Even though I can see the hint of hesitation in her eyes, she is happy I am here.

"Ah, the long lost twins reunite. See, I wasn't being too much of a lunatic. It really looks like mine."

"Well, you did chase me down, scream at me, and almost have me arrested, so I wouldn't say you're sane either."

"True. It wasn't my finest moment. But I have taken down the 'Wanted' posters I plastered up all over the airport now that I've realized my mistake. My apologies if you get tackled on your way out."

I smile at her, take off my coat, and sling it across my arm. "Perhaps I should keep you with me for a bit, you know, just so you can set the record straight in case I'm questioned again. Care to grab a bite?" I nod at the pub next to us.

Her eyes grow big and then quickly recover. "Oh, that's very kind of you, but I'm waiting for my ride. Should be here any minute. I'm just inside because it's too cold out there."

"Oh, come on, you owe me one. Don't make a poor acquitted thief eat alone when he's across the country by himself. You can give me pointers on Connecticut. Tell me some good places to visit while I'm here. I'm Gabe, by the way." I reach out my hand.

"Callie." She shakes my hand and in that brief instant I feel something stir deep in my chest; it's electric and unexpected.

It takes me fully by surprise. I don't think I've ever felt so drawn to a woman like this before, especially since I know absolutely nothing about her.

I wonder if she feels it, too.

But I can see she is hesitating and doesn't want to let her guard down. She undoubtedly thinks I'm crazy for asking her to eat with me after what just happened.

"Nice to meet you, Callie. Let's grab a drink. You owe me at least that after nearly getting me crushed by Gus, the Green Giant."

I'm not perfect, and I'm not beneath using a guilt trip to get an intriguing woman to have a drink with me.

"Oh, now that's not fair! And I like to think of him as Grumpy Gus, thank you very much."

I fake a scared shiver and frown at her, laying it on thick.

"I'm still a bit shook up. Everyone was looking at me, staring. That security guard was huge. I'll probably have nightmares tonight. I may need to see a therapist."

"You're relentless." She smiles, but still looks suspicious of me. "Fine, one drink. But I'm not in the mood to tell my life story or do the thing where we share our sad past at the bar, ok? Just a drink. Nothing more. Deal?"

"Deal." I grin and help her up, following her into the bar where we find a couple of empty seats.

"You don't look very tan for being in Jamaica," I say.

"You don't look very tan for being from California."

"Touché."

I order a beer and Callie chooses a glass of pinot noir, which I know to be awful, but in her defense there isn't much on the menu.

"So what brought you to Jamaica? Business or pleasure?"

"Let's not talk about my trip," she says, deflecting. "What brings you to Connecticut?"

Jamaica is obviously a sore spot.

"I'm here to look at a building I own and sign off on the sale of it."

"Can't you do that from California?"

"Yes, but I've never seen it in person, so I wanted to see it one time before it's gone."

"Well, that's unusual. You bought a building sight unseen?" She seems to relax with the focus on me.

"No, my grandfather left me the building in his will." I take a sip of my beer. "I've held onto it for a while. The man who was leasing it closed his business and my realtor is having trouble renting it out again, so I think it's best to sell."

"Is it hard for you to let it go?"

"Yes. Knowing that he wanted it to stay in the family makes it hard to feel good about selling it. That's the reason I've held onto it for so long. I wasn't even aware he lived in Connecticut when he was younger until he died."

In fact, it had come as quite a shock when my grandfather left me the building in his will. Out of all his assets, I had heard nothing mentioned about a property in Connecticut. Of course, there was the vineyard, the wine shops, and the rental units, all in California, and all of those were left to my mother. But I had known about those and grew up being part of the family business since I was a little kid. I always just assumed my grandfather Dominic had lived his entire life in California.

When he died, the attorney read us the will and said the Hopemeadow building was left to me because it held a special place in his heart. The reason for that remains a mystery to me.

"Was he living here while on business?"

"I'm not sure. My mother said he lived here for about a year, well before she was born and before he married my grandmother. Apparently, he purchased the property right before he left. She said it had some sentimental value to him, but she never understood why he refused to sell it."

It bothers me not knowing why he abruptly moved across the country and uprooted his life. There has to be a story there; no one does that without a reason. Now it seems like I will never learn what happened.

"I can see why that must have been a tough decision for you to make. At least you get to see it first."

"Yeah, from the photos I've seen, it looks like it has nice bones, but it makes little sense for me to hold on to it anymore or sink money into it. I plan on using the proceeds from the sale to fund an investment opportunity I've been looking into. My Gramps was a businessman, so I think he would like that."

She nods, glancing again at her phone. I know she is waiting on a ride, but I don't want to let on that I had been eavesdropping earlier. I order a couple appetizers for us to pick at and excuse myself to the restroom.

When I come back, a large man with a shaved head, who looks to be about 6'4" with many visible tattoos, is sitting in my seat next to Callie. He is leaning in a bit too close and she is clearly not wanting to talk to him.

I walk over just in time to hear him say, "… oh come on honey, give a guy a chance. You'll like me once you get to know me. And once you like me, you'll love me." The line oozes slime and I can tell by her face she is not enjoying his attention.

"Sorry, I have a boyfriend," she says, trying to turn away from him.

"Boyfriend? I don't see any boyfriend. What he doesn't know won't hurt him. I'll get you a shot. On me."

I take that as my cue. "Callie, darling. Is this a friend of yours?" I look her in the eye, hoping she will play along. I stand next to her barstool and wrap my arm around her waist, pulling her close to my side.

Feeling her pressed against me sends a jolt through my body. I can smell her shampoo, something floral and sweet I can't place, and the soft warmth of her has me reeling.

How a complete stranger can continue to have this effect on me is unnerving, to say the least.

And I'm loving every minute of it.

At first the guy looks annoyed and then squints his eyes, trying to assess me.

"Hi honey," she says. "He was just leaving." She glares at him, not hesitating to show her disdain.

"Oh good, because that's my seat you're in."

He looks me up and down and then over at Callie.

"Yeah, I was just leaving." He walks off annoyed and heads back to the end of the bar.

Callie sighs, frustrated. "Why do guys think it's ok to just touch you and invade your space?"

"I didn't mean to make you uncomfortable. He didn't look

like he was taking the hint, so I thought it was best to be convincing."

She laughs. "Not you, Gabe. That I appreciated. Nice save." She reaches over and touches my arm gently. "I was talking about him. He just came over uninvited and wouldn't take a hint. He's still staring over here. Maybe we should keep up the ruse a bit longer. Pretend to like me and that I'm not the woman who almost had you arrested, ok?"

I smile, relieved. "That shouldn't be too hard to do." I signal to the bartender to bring us two more drinks. "If you were my girlfriend, I'd probably be sitting closer. More like this." I move my barstool next to hers so there is little space between us.

"How scandalous, Gabe. Why, our knees are almost touching," she teases.

"I know, it's hard for ladies to resist my bold moves. Try not to be swayed." The bartender comes back with our drinks and food. I know I was starving, but now? Suddenly, it's the last thing on my mind. "If I'm being honest, I'd probably find a reason to get even closer and pretend I have a secret to tell you. Like this." I lean in and lightly graze my cheek against hers and whisper in her ear. "I'd say something like, you're the most beautiful woman I've ever seen. How did I get so lucky?"

I feel her shiver a little and pull back to see her cheeks redden. I grin, knowing I have at least some effect on her.

Maybe she is feeling it, too.

"Ok, easy killer. I get the picture now."

"I don't know if you've noticed, but we're under mistletoe." I point up to the mistletoe that dangles above every other seat at the bar. Callie looks up and rolls her eyes.

"Ugh, don't get me started on mistletoe. Why would a bar do that? It's like they're looking for trouble."

I shake my head, chuckling in disbelief. "Wait, there has to be a story behind this. You have something against mistletoe? It's a holiday classic. It's romantic."

"How in the world is mistletoe romantic? Do you know anything about mistletoe?"

"I feel like this is a trap."

"I'm not kidding! Mistletoe is evil."

"Evil?" I burst out laughing. "Ok, enlighten me. How is mistletoe evil?"

"Everyone thinks that it's some cutesy tradition, but it has allowed shady, unwanted advances on women for hundreds of years. Did you know women were told if they refused the kiss they would have bad luck? So they only agreed out of fear."

"Maybe that's how it started, but it has evolved into something sweet. It's pretty innocent now."

"Even the real plant itself is awful. It's a parasite. It grows on other plants and destroys them. How it continues to be a symbol of love and affection is beyond me."

"Wow, Callie. That's... something," I say, shaking my head, amused.

"What?"

"Maybe instead of looking for the bad, you can think about the positives. Mistletoe can bloom during the coldest winter. Mistletoe is a fighter. Can't fault something for being tenacious and going after what it needs."

"It's invasive. It takes what it wants and doesn't care what it hurts along the way. Same with the kissing tradition. If I want to kiss someone, I don't need to be under a plant for that to happen. Plus, every time I'm near mistletoe something bad happens. It's a curse."

"Sheez, Callie, you're pretty cynical, aren't you? Who hurt you?"

I am joking and laugh as I say this, but, by the look on her face, it is obvious someone had.

CHAPTER 4

CALLIE - 24 HOURS AGO

ONE OF THE MOST ROMANTIC PLACES IN THE WORLD IS NOW THE last place I want to be. I long to lie on the beach with a cold drink in my hand and listen to the swell of the ocean. Maybe even dig my toes in the sand and read a book.

But this is anything but relaxing. Jake planned non-stop activities and excursions around the island. And not "day-at-the-spa-pampering" type activities. That would have been wonderful.

Since the minute we landed, it has felt like I am on an adventure game show where we have to cram in as many thrill seeking activities as possible. I am many things, but an adrenaline junkie is not one of them. I'm terrified of heights. I get anxiety in glass elevators. Even running low on gas can give me a stomachache. Those shows always end up with someone being forced to eat some slimy, exotic bug. I am half expecting him to announce that's what is next for us.

He arranged for us to parasail in the morning and zipline in the afternoon. I had zero desire to do any of it, but he had already paid for it all in advance. He said he was trying to make this surprise trip special for me.

If by special, he meant panic inducing, then sure.

My nerves are shot.

We just got back to the resort from ziplining and we barely talked on the ride back. I lay splayed out like a starfish on the bed, trying to compose myself.

"I have one more surprise planned for tonight," Jake says as he digs through his suitcase, tossing clothes everywhere.

"Please, no more surprises. I'm so tired. I don't think I can handle any more excitement. Can we just take it easy tonight and hang out here? I saw there was a reggae band playing in the lobby tonight."

"No way! It's dead here. You'll love this place we're going."

"Jake…"

"No, I promise, Callie. I know some things we did today weren't your favorite…"

"Understatement of the year," I grumble. "You know I hate things like that. What were you thinking? You said we would relax on this trip and we haven't sat on the beach once!"

Jake promised me we'd be beach bums on this long weekend in Jamaica. He said it would be a much needed opportunity to relax. Relaxing is tough for me in general, but especially this time of year. The timing of the trip stunned me; he knew this trip was just days before the annual Hopemeadow Holiday Festival. Why couldn't he plan this for January after the mad holiday rush at the bakery was over? He knows how much effort goes into making the spread for that event and the many others I have lined up over the next few weeks. December is my busiest time of year at the bakery.

But Jake insisted I was burning myself out. I think the words he used were, "You're too uptight. You need to loosen up and enjoy your life for a change."

After I got over the sting of that jab, I agreed to go and started looking forward to it. He's right; I haven't taken a vacation in years and I've never been to Jamaica. I spent the next few weeks deciding which books I wanted to bring and ordered a new bathing suit. By the time we left, I was grateful for the getaway and thought about surprising him with a couples massage as a thank you.

But what is happening now? This is not what I signed up for.

"This has been relaxing! And fun! You sounded like you were enjoying yourself on the zipline." He changes out of one Hawaiian shirt and into another that looks eerily similar.

Jake without a shirt is easy to look at and reminds me of one of the reasons I agreed to date him in the first place: he's gorgeous. Jake is tall, blonde, and has the physique of a surfer with broad shoulders and a defined stomach. Spending his days as a contractor keeps him in incredible shape and in the off season he fills his free time at the gym. He's kind and funny, and he really is a good guy. But I'm starting to realize that beyond my appreciation for his looks, I'm not sure if we have anything in common.

"That wasn't me enjoying myself. I was screaming my face off in terror."

He laughs. "Stop, it wasn't that bad. Trust me, you'll love this café we're going to tonight."

"A café?" Jake isn't a laid back café kind of guy. That's more my thing. He's finally thinking about me and what I'd like! Maybe I'm just being impatient today. I prop myself up and say, "A café would be great."

"Yeah, and it's apparently on the cliffs in Negril and has a great view of the sunset. The food is supposed to be decent, too. And I know how much you love boats, so I scheduled one to take us over."

I sit up completely now and grin. I'm thrilled. "That sounds wonderful. I'm in."

A half hour later, we are packed like sardines on a catamaran thumping with party music and are being served watered down, overpriced drinks. I focus on the spectacular view around us and can't wait to get to the café so we can relax together and watch the sunset.

But the minute we step off the catamaran, I realize the word café is not appropriate for this place. Joe's Café is a giant, tourist filled bar. He is right about one thing, though; the view is stunning. If we can find a place to sit and relax, seeing the sunset here would be amazing.

"Callie! Look at this place. It's incredible."

"It's something, alright." I try to keep up as he zig-zags his way through the crowd to the hostess station. I give up trying to push my way through, so I lag behind and wait towards the back next to the bar. Joe's is everything I try to avoid when I travel, but the band is amazing. I close my eyes and listen to the Bob Marley cover.

You're right, Bob. Every little thing, gonna be alright. I'm on vacation, time to enjoy it.

Jake finally makes his way back to me. "Babe, they said it's about a 90 minute wait for a table, so I put our name on the list. Did you see the other line over there? That's for cliff jumping! Let's go!"

I turn to look and there are throngs of people in their swimsuits, all drinking and chatting in lines that snake down all the way back towards the bar. I look back towards the front of the line and watch a young guy gear up and propel himself over the side of the cliff, going down like a pencil.

It must be at least a 30 foot drop.

"You've got to be kidding me. You know I'm afraid of heights. There's no way I'm doing that!"

"Come on! You'll love it. Live a little!"

"Jake, no. I have no interest in cliff jumping. Plus, I'm not even wearing my bathing suit. I thought we were coming here to have dinner. When you said café, this wasn't what I was expecting."

"Suit yourself. Just come wait with me in line then."

"I'm starving. Is there any way we can go somewhere else?" I plead. "It looks like there are a couple smaller places up the road. I bet there are less people and we might be able to actually hear each other."

"No way! This place is amazing. We're already here. Let's just make the most of it."

I don't want to cause a scene and fight in front of people, so I give up. "You go ahead. I'll stay here in case they call our name for the table and watch the band."

"Alright. Keep an eye out and when you see me get to the front of the line come take a picture of me jumping."

He doesn't wait for me to respond and bee-lines it towards the line without even so much as a glance behind him.

An hour later, as Jake makes his way through the line to jump for a second time, I sit on the edge of the water near the catamaran, watching the sun slowly sink into the ocean. It is unlike anything I have ever seen before. This bar may be a tourist trap, but the sunset is worth it.

The warm breeze blows in as I gaze out at the water lapping and crashing in on the beach in front of me. It is gorgeous here, and even though I am supposed to be on a romantic vacation with my boyfriend, I am happy to be watching this spectacular moment alone. This entire trip feels wrong, and I have a sinking feeling Jake and I will never be the same.

I wish I was sharing this beautiful moment with someone else. Someone who understands me, supports me, and who truly loves me. Jake only seems to care about himself. Why drag me here for us to do things apart? Why only plan activities he knows he would love and I would hate? I don't understand why he would bring me here at all.

And it is so out of character for him to make such a grand gesture like this. I felt like I couldn't say no to this trip (not to mention he said he purchased non-refundable tickets). For all of our problems, and there are many, at least this showed he cares and is trying.

I persuade a passing server to bring me a Red Stripe and an appetizer while I wait for the table. Just as my jerk chicken kabobs arrive, Jake saunters back over, wet and smiling, and grabs one from my plate. I am so hungry, he's lucky he didn't pull back a stub.

"You obviously knew to wear *your* swimsuit. How lucky," I say sarcastically.

"It's Jamaica, mon. Gotta be prepared. There are so many interesting people here. I met professional cliff jumpers in line. They actually do this for a living!"

Jake continues on about the cliff jumpers and how they must lead such an exciting life. I can't understand why he envies them. Jake is doing great and slowly moving up the ranks at J&M Construction. He's talented and seems to love his job, but, admittedly, he doesn't make a lot of money. That never mattered to me, but I'm pretty sure it bothers him that I make more money than he does. We can't even talk about the success of the bakery without him looking annoyed and changing the topic. I am by no means rich, but I am proud of how far the business has come. I don't want to be ashamed of my success.

The whole thing is wearing on me. We make a little more small talk and then sit in silence, waiting for the check.

I know I should end it. This isn't the time or the place for that, but it is becoming so painfully obvious on this trip I can't take it anymore. I don't want to sit and pretend. I want to be home, back in Hopemeadow. I'm not overworked. I *love* my job. I love the bakery. I love the holidays and don't want to spend it on a beach. I love everything about my life, but as much as it pains me to admit it to myself, I don't love Jake. But for some reason, I keep trying to change myself to please him. Why am I trying to force this relationship to work?

When we return to the resort, Jake says he is going to the

bar, and I retreat to our room alone so I can shower and go to bed.

As I let the water wash over me, so does the guilt.

Jake tried to make an effort. He spent so much money on this trip. Seeing as it is his off-season at work, he isn't getting a paycheck. Splurging on a trip like this is a big deal for him. He must have dipped into his savings to afford it, which means the new truck he has been wanting will take even longer to get.

I need to stop overthinking everything and just go back to the bar and enjoy this trip with him. He's trying. I should try harder, right? What's a relationship if there isn't some give and take? I can give more of my time and do things he wants to do.

I rush to get dressed and just as I am on my way out the door, the phone in the room rings.

"Hello?"

"Ms. Parker?"

"Yes, this is she."

"Hi, this is Jayden at the front desk. I'm calling to let you know your card has been declined and we need to secure a new method of payment."

"There must be a mistake. That can't be possible. Can you please try to run it again?"

"I'm sorry, we attempted it twice. It was declined both times."

Flustered, I dig through my bag, grab another card, and read him the numbers.

"That worked. Thanks so much and I apologize for the confusion. I hope you are enjoying your stay. If there is anything we can do for you, please don't hesitate to give the front desk a call."

I hang up in a panic. I gave them my card at check in while Jake was bringing our bags to the room. How could I have maxed it out already? This doesn't make any sense. I haven't paid for anything yet! I flip open my laptop and sign into my account to check to see what purchases I have accrued, praying my card number hasn't been stolen.

It takes only a moment to realize what is going on. I am instantly flooded with anger.

On my card are the charges for the flight to Jamaica, as well as all the excursions from today, and several for tomorrow, all made by Jake.

I unwittingly funded this trip.

I drop into the chair at the desk in disbelief. I can't believe he did this.

I gave Jake my credit card number a long time ago just so he could put our dinners or other small purchases on it when we needed something. On and off, I would see a small charge here or there that we didn't discuss, but it wasn't a big deal. He always paid it back and I always trusted him.

Until now.

I slam my laptop shut, grab my room key, and make my way towards the resort bar. How could he do this to me? He made it seem like he paid for this trip. What gives him the right to do this without talking to me first??

I round the corner and stop dead in my tracks. Jake is on the dance floor, slow dancing with another woman. She is tall, with sleek shoulder-length blonde hair, and is wearing a half shirt and a barely there skirt. Even without seeing her face, without knowing her, I know she is everything I'm not. She is the thrill seeker. The fun one who is up for anything. Not the woman who can't relax because she is so eager to get home to her business.

I back away, forcing myself to take deep breaths. I have to get out of here. This trip is over.

And so were we.

CHAPTER 5

CALLIE

"Sheez, Callie, you're pretty cynical, aren't you? Who hurt you?" Gabe jokes.

I hesitate, not knowing what to say. Gabe is a nice guy, but he's a complete stranger. I'm never going to see him again. Why get into what happened? We already said we wouldn't share our sad stories.

"Let's just say I haven't had the best luck with relationships," I say slowly.

"Fair enough. But that just means you haven't met the right guy yet."

I laugh. "Wow, do you really believe all this? Are you that optimistic about everything?"

"Sure. You can't control what other people do, but you can control how you react to things."

"Ok, so what about you? Have you had any bad relationships?"

"Ah, I see. Change the subject so we're no longer talking about you, right?"

I raise my eyebrows and look at him. "Isn't that *you* deflecting?"

"You're a pro, Callie. Fine, I'll take the bait. Yes, I have. I've had relationships that weren't right and didn't work out. I've been burned. But I learned something from each of them. I've had my heart broken, but looking back I can see it had to happen."

"Wow. Your girlfriend must be so happy to be with such a well-adjusted guy…" I hope my leading question isn't too obvious, but even I hear it for what it really is.

He leans in and grins. "Is that your way of asking me if I'm single?"

"No, I'm just commenting on your super uplifting approach to relationships," I blurt, embarrassed. "You don't have to answer."

"I've got nothing to hide. There's no girlfriend at the moment. I'm single, unless you count the five minute relationship I had with you to fend off Mr. Clean down there." He nods down to the guy at the bar who is now attempting to pick up another woman seated at a nearby table. She doesn't look pleased. "And what about you?"

"Same."

For less than a day, but who's counting?

"Is it because you told the last one you hate mistletoe and all romantic things at Christmas?"

I laugh. "No, although now that you mention it, I'm sure that doesn't help. I will leave that out of any first date conversations from here on out."

The corners of his lips hitch. "Callie, are you saying this is our first date?"

Flustered, I stammer, "No, n-n-o. That's not what I meant. I meant when I go on a date, you know, at another time… not this current time…"

He chuckles and touches my hand. "Relax. I'm just messing with you."

I look down at his hand and when I look up, our eyes lock.

He has the most gentle blue eyes, and the heat from his touch makes my stomach flip. I can feel it clear to my toes. I bite my lip and feel my breath go ragged.

Snap out of it! What are you doing?

I pull my hand away. I don't even know this man, and I'm newly single. No more guys to distract me.

My phone vibrates on the bar and I lunge at it. It's a text from Jules.

CALLIE! Don't hate me! I fell asleep watching The Holiday on the couch. I'm digging the car out now, but we got dumped on. There's like 6 inches already and it's coming down like crazy. It's going to be at least another hour until I get there. I'm so sorry! I'll be there, ASAP!

"UGH, COME ON, JULES," I mutter to myself.

I have to get out of here and get home. I have so much work to do to prepare for the Hopemeadow Annual Christmas Festival, and here I am sitting at a bar flirting with a stranger.

"Everything ok?"

"No, my ride just texted me and she's saying she won't be here for over an hour. I have so much I have to do..."

"What is it you do, exactly?"

I hesitate and decide to be vague, but honest. "I own my own business."

"Impressive." I search his face and find that he means it. He truly is impressed, which is a nice change of pace from someone being threatened by it.

Which reminds me of the whole swearing off all men thing. Why do I care what he thinks?

"Actually, I have a huge event coming up I should be home prepping for. I'm sorry, it was nice meeting you, but I have to go."

I stand up and grab my purse, digging for my wallet to pay the bill.

"Oh, don't worry about it. It's on me." He places a few bills on the bar and looks disappointed. "I wish you didn't have to run off so soon. I have to grab my rental, and you would need to direct me, but can I drop you somewhere?"

"Thank you, but no, I will catch a taxi. You've been so kind and a good distraction tonight. Sorry again about the mix up."

Gabe stands and grabs my luggage, rolling it towards me. He is much taller than me and because we pushed our bar stools so close together we are now mere inches apart. I instantly feel drawn to him and can smell the faint allure of his cologne. I imagine what it would be like to have his arms around me. For him to lean down and be close enough to breathe him in...

What is wrong with me?! I just got out of a relationship!

He looks down and I can see he is torn about what to do. It is almost as if he is hesitating and wanting to say something but can't. I speak up before he has a chance.

"Yeah, so good luck with everything. Have a great time in Connecticut! Bye, Gabe."

I walk towards the door to leave and when I am almost out of the bar, he jogs after me to catch up. Surprised, I turned around.

"What's wrong? Did I accidentally take your luggage this time?"

He laughs. "Not this time. I'll walk you out. I might as well grab my rental car and head out too."

I nod, unsure what to say, and keep walking towards the exit.

"Say I wanted to get in touch with you while I'm here. How would I do that?"

"Gabe..."

"I only have a few things I need to take care of, so I'll have some down time and maybe I could come take you out for coffee. I feel like I need more time to convince you on the merits of mistletoe."

I stop at the taxi station just as one pulls up.

"Look, you seem like a great guy, but I think it's best that we leave tonight as is. Meeting you was certainly…memorable." I smile up at him and walk towards the cab, immediately wondering if I'm making a mistake.

Before I know what is happening, he grabs my arm and, in one fluid motion, pulls me back to face him. I'm inches from him and he lifts my chin with his hand.

"Hey! What the…" I protest.

But the minute I look into his eyes, all arguments in my mind fall apart.

What I find there isn't just heat. It's an uncanny sense of coming home, which makes absolutely no sense. This man is a complete stranger, yet, somehow, with this one look, it feels like I've known him forever.

It's mesmerizing and I can't look away.

A moment passes and, when he speaks, his voice is strong, but rough. "I'm disappointed there's no mistletoe out here."

I'm at a loss for words as he gently tucks an errant strand of hair behind my ear. His hand continues lightly down my cheek, and his gaze falls to my mouth as he lightly runs his thumb over my lips.

I'm frozen still. My rational side is telling me I should leave, except for this place deep down screaming there is nowhere else I'd rather be.

What I say surprises me in both its forwardness and honesty. It's barely a whisper. "I already told you, I don't need mistletoe if I want to kiss someone."

A grin tugs at the corner of his lips. "Thank goodness for that."

He leans in and kisses me with a deep, slow urgency. I kiss him back, wrapping my arms around his shoulders, and lean into him. I am dizzy with surprise and the jolt of heat coursing through me.

When he pulls away, I stare at him, stunned and breathless. He smiles, taking my hand, and leads me to the cab idling at the curb. He opens the door for me and stands aside so I can get in, handing my suitcase to the driver to place in the trunk.

Before he closes the door, he leans down. "It was a pleasure meeting you, Callie. An absolute pleasure."

I touch my lips, still reeling from his kiss, as he waves, and the cab pulls away.

CHAPTER 6

GABE

I T IS MIDNIGHT BEFORE I ARRIVE AT THE HILLSIDE INN. THE DRIVE there is slow with the snow, but even at night the town of Hope-meadow looks like it has sprung to life out of a painting. It is quintessential New England, with one small strip of businesses in the heart of town and nestled on the side of a mountain. I am tired, but can't get Callie out of my mind as I make my way up the long, winding road towards the inn.

I pull up to a large lodge surrounded by a series of smaller cabins, all spread out separately around it. The main lodge is dark, and it dawns on me that I might not be able to check in, or have a place to stay, if they already shut down for the night. I walk up to the door and find it is locked. I curse to myself, but then notice a note taped lower on the door along with an enve-lope that contains a key:

MR. MONTGOMERY,

I couldn't stay up to wait for you any longer. A phone call would have been nice. You'll be staying in cabin 5 behind the main lodge. Yours is the one with the reindeer wreath on the door. Breakfast is available in the lodge starting at 7:00 am and ends promptly at 10:00 am.

SLEEP WELL,
   Doris Winkleblack

FROM THE SOUND of that note, I'll likely be on the receiving end of a stern talking to on manners at breakfast in the morning.

I look around. There doesn't appear to be any other guests staying in the cabins. All is dark and the parking lot is empty. It surprises me that the owner would feel it is safe to leave a key out in plain view, but I am starting to realize Hopemeadow is much different from what I'm used to back home.

The cabin I rented is quaint. It is one large room with an eat-in kitchen and a small table on one side, and a fireplace with an intimate seating area on the other. The king sized bed is in the back corner and only separated from the rest of the space by a large room divider. The bed is layered in flannel sheets and a down comforter, making it look warm and inviting. But as comfortable and well appointed as it seems, the cabin is utterly freezing. I get to work starting the fire and, once I have it going, I take a moment to sit and get warm.

In the fire's glow, my mind wanders back to Callie. There was something about her that stuck me in a way no other woman has before. Yes, she is unbelievably beautiful, but not in a conventional way. She is curvy in all the right places, with a heart-shaped face, and cheeks that turned the sweetest shade of pink when she is flustered. Her smile is infectious, and I love how she unapologetically spoke her mind. She seemed feisty and driven, and nothing is more attractive than a confident woman.

Yet, what struck me the most is how it felt to look into her warm, hazel eyes; it was familiar but new at the same time. My tendency to indulge my impulses led me to kiss her, and now that I have, I regret that I didn't push harder to get her number. Having no way to contact her kills me. I don't know her last name, the name of her business, or where she lives in Connecticut.

Nothing.

It's probably for the best, though. I shouldn't be chasing after a woman who lives across the country when my life is in California. I need to stay focused on why I'm here, finalize the sale, and head home as soon as possible.

I lay on the bed and drift off to sleep, trying hard to not recall the sweet taste of her mouth and the feeling of her soft lips on mine.

"Ah, you must be Mr. Montgomery. I'm Doris Winkleblack. Welcome to Hopemeadow." Doris greets me in the lobby with a warm smile. She looks like the stereotypical sweet little grandmother that everyone needs in their life. She is a small woman with perfectly white hair nestled up into a bun at the crown of her head. Her red, chunky cardigan hangs on her slight frame and oversized glasses dangle by a string around her neck. By all appearances, especially considering this time of year, she could easily be mistaken for Mrs. Claus.

"Nice to meet you. Please, call me Gabe."

"Did you enjoy your first night with us?"

"Yes, thank you very much. The cabin is perfect. I apologize for not giving you a heads up that I would be arriving so late. I think they delayed many flights because of the storm."

"Bygones, young man. The coffee and tea are set up over there and I have some pancakes I can bring out for you."

I breathe a sigh of relief. It appears that I won't be receiving a lecture about the night before. I can step up to the biggest man in the room and not back down, but little old ladies intimidate the heck out of me. I think of them all like my grandmother. She was no joke. You did not mess with that woman.

"That would be great, thanks."

She disappears into the kitchen and comes out rolling a cart filled with an extensive breakfast spread, including pancakes, bacon, fruit, toast, and jams. Doris arranges it carefully on the table.

"Is there anything else I can get for you, Gabe?"

"No, this looks wonderful. Thank you so much."

She brings some orange juice and a carafe of water and places it on the table in front of me. "So, what brings you to Hopemeadow? We don't get too many visitors here around the holidays that aren't family."

"I'm here on business. I own a building in town that I'm selling."

Suddenly, she seems very interested and settles into a seat at the table with me. "Really? What building?"

I pour myself some orange juice and pile a stack of pancakes in front of me. It smells incredible. "Where Lou's Trinkets and Treasures used to be. Do you know the place?"

"Oh my! Of course! You're the owner of Lou's old place?"

"Yes. My grandfather left it to me when he passed. Since Lou closed shop, we haven't been able to rent out the space because it needs a lot of work, but we've recently had an interested party contact us about selling. I figured it was time."

Doris nods solemnly. "Yes, I know about Lou retiring. He's been having trouble with his health for the past few years."

"That's too bad. Hopefully he can enjoy his retirement now." I take a sip of my orange juice and without thinking add, "Apparently a regional franchise owner thinks Hopemeadow would be a great location to expand their bakery. A place called Bon Bon's. Have you heard of it?"

"Bon Bon's wants to open up here in Hopemeadow? Why, that cannot happen!" she exclaims as she stands up, disturbed by the revelation. "We already have a wonderful bakery and it's right next door to Lou's old place. That young lady took it over from her grandmother. We don't want a chain here. No. No, thank you."

"Oh." I pause, realizing I struck a nerve and mentally kicking myself for oversharing. I should have known better; you never know who you're talking to in a small town like this. "Well, nothing's final. Since we put it on the market, there are a few other interested buyers, as well. I'm just in town to see the sale through and visit the building before it sells. My grandfather lived here years ago, so I thought I owed it to him to see it once."

She grabs her glasses that are dangling at her chest. "Your grandfather?" She slides them on, drawing close, and squints at me for a better look. With a flash of realization, she smiles broadly and puts her hand over her heart. "I thought you looked familiar! Was your grandfather's name Dominick?"

"Yes! Did you know him?"

"You look just like him. I remember him well. He was here for a short time. He was such a good man."

"Thank you. He certainly was." I realize this is my chance to find out more about his time here. "This may seem like an odd question, but do you happen to know why he was here? Or what made him leave? His time in Hopemeadow is a bit of a mystery in my family."

"Why, of course! He was..."

At that moment, a stumpy man with a beer belly and worn denim overalls bursts into the lobby and loudly exclaims, "Morning, Doris! The dang sink is leaking in cabin 4! It made a mess of the rug."

Doris stands up, looking distressed. "Oh dear, it is? Again? I thought you fixed that last week!"

"That was the shower in cabin 2. I told you some of the

plumbing here was going to have issues." He realizes I'm here and stops. "Who's your guest?"

"This is Gabe Montgomery. He owns Lou's old building. Gabe, this is Hank."

"Well, I'll be! Nice to meet you, Gabe! You coming to shape up that old building? That thing is a beaut' but needs a little work. I'm a handy man around here and I'd be glad to help if you have a thing or two that needs fixing."

Recalling how Doris reacted to my news of the impending sale, I dodge the question.

"Nice to meet you too and thanks for the offer."

"Now Doris, I need to talk to you about those pipes... "

Hank and Doris excuse themselves to the back to discuss the plumbing issue. I continue with breakfast alone and realize, with Doris's help, I might finally find out more about my grandfather.

As I am getting up to leave, Doris and Hank come back out, still in the middle of discussing the best way to fix the sink. I have back-to-back conference calls this morning, but I need to make sure I arrange a time to sit down with her.

"Doris, I know you're busy, but I'd love to chat with you later about my grandfather."

"Yes! That sounds lovely. Are you going to the festival tonight? We could head over together!"

"I was planning on staying in tonight to get some work done, but I'd be happy to meet you here in the lobby before you go."

"Oh Gabe, I'm sorry, I cannot allow that to happen! You can't miss the annual Hopemeadow Holiday Festival! It is the one event I look forward to the most each year. Everything is deco-rated for Christmas and the Holly Hop is such fun! It's at Kiel-ty's pub again this year. Plus, there is the parade and you'll love all the special events around Main Street."

None of that means anything to me, but I know she isn't

going to let this go. How can I say no to an excited little old lady?

"I guess I could head into town with you for a bit. Can we talk there?"

"Absolutely! Meet me here in the lobby at 6." She smiles and then her face turns disapproving. "We can also discuss that building of yours. The nice young lady whose business you're about to ruin is catering the event. Perhaps if you see it yourself, you will change your mind."

CHAPTER 7

"Jules! I think we're good with the cookie and pastry platters for now. I'm going to keep a few backups in the cooler just in case we run low again this year. If we don't use them tonight, we can pull them for the treat truck at ice skating."

I've been working nonstop to make sure everything is ready for the annual Hopemeadow Holiday Festival. This particular event is one of my favorites because it kicks off the Christmas season in town. The community always goes above and beyond to make Christmas magical.

All traffic on Main Street is shut down and everyone pours into the street enjoying a variety of holiday themed events. Sam from the deli takes this opportunity to dust off his magic routine for the kids. The local dance troupes and children's choir that have been practicing for months always perform. I'm a judge in the gingerbread house decorating contest each year, and I can't wait to see what the families submitted. They are always so creative.

The most anticipated event is the fire truck parade, which ends with Santa Claus coming into town, waving and throwing candy from an intricately decorated fire truck. As soon as the parade is over, Santa (played by Mayor Collins) is dropped at Johnson's grocery store to be the official master of ceremony for the town tree lighting and a spectacular fireworks show.

Most local businesses pitch in to sponsor an event, and I've always sent our treat truck out to park in front of the library. Over the last few years Honey's has become an integral part of the festival and, on the heels of my awful trip, I am ready for some positivity and good cheer. Bring on all the holiday spirit, Hopemeadow.

Jules is just about finished taking care of the last of the dishes at the sink and is dancing along to an imaginary beat. Her shoulder length caramel brown hair bounces up and down as she bops her head from side to side. She must have her earphones in again because she doesn't answer me when I call her name. I love how she always brings positive energy with her. Only Jules can make doing the dishes fun.

"Earth to Jules!" I walk over and tap her on her shoulder. She jumps dramatically and yelps.

"Ahh! You scared me half to death! You can't sneak up on me like that."

"I didn't sneak up on you! Half the time I'm here talking to myself because you're in another world with those earphones."

"Well, maybe if the conversation was a little more interesting, I wouldn't need them." She leans towards me eagerly. "I know. You could tell me why you came back from Jamaica early and why Jake is blowing up the phone here."

Jake has been trying to reach me nonstop since I left Jamaica, and I've been avoiding him. Today, he resorted to bombarding the bakery with calls. I have nothing to say to him and don't want to waste any more time on him. Even the idea of rehashing the whole thing with Jules exhausts me. I don't want to think about it anymore. I just want it all to be over.

"There's not much to tell. We're done. I left early. He clearly hasn't taken the hint."

"Oh, come on!" She puts the last dish in the dishwasher and turns it on. "You guys are together for months, you go away on a romantic vacation, and then it's suddenly over? There's definitely a story here."

I say nothing, but silence doesn't stop Jules. I should know better by now.

"What did he do? When it ended, did you throw a drink in his face? Did he wear one too many Hawaiian shirts and it drove you to the edge?"

I laugh and shake my head. "Jules! I don't want to get into it right now." I take a breath and rub my eyes. "Things happened you can't bounce back from. Worse than the awful shirts. I just want to enjoy tonight and not think about it, ok?"

"Ugh, fine. You're going to tell me eventually though, you know that, right?"

"Yes. We can talk about it at girls' night. Just not tonight. There's so much going on and I still need to get dressed and set everything up. I keep going over my notes to make sure we have enough on hand for each station."

"Callie, we're good! You're always so prepared. You've got back ups for your back ups." She takes off her apron and tosses it on the counter beside her. "Tonight will be great. It always is. You should relax and enjoy yourself. Would you like me to set up and run the cocoa station this year? Then you can just man the station at the Holly Hop and mingle with everyone while Cameron handles the treat truck."

We received rave reviews last year for the cocoa and cookies station we set up for the kids visiting Santa at town hall and at the treat truck we parked at the library. This year, Mayor Collins asked me to cater an additional location and provide a dessert table for the Holly Hop at Kielty's pub. I am stretching it with my limited staff and space at the bakery, but I couldn't say no.

The Holly Hop is a Hopemeadow tradition that goes back 70

years. Each year the pub hires a band to come play old school holiday music and the second the band starts all the seniors fill the dance floor. It is adorable.

"That sounds good. I'll touch base with Cameron and make sure the truck is set to go before I leave. Do you think the dress I got from Lana's shop will work?"

Normally, I'd layer tons of warm clothes for running the treat truck or cocoa station, but the Hop is an adults only, more formal event than the rest of the festivities.

"Oh! The beautiful red dress that flares out at the knee? Yes!! It looks so gorgeous on you." Jules is not only my right hand at the bakery, but she is also my best friend who always knows the right thing to say to boost my confidence.

I smile. "Thanks. And thanks for being patient with me lately. I know I've been all over the map. I just need to regain my footing. I let things with Jake distract me too much and I know it impacted things here. I'm sorry."

"I just want you to be happy, Callie." She lowers her voice in earnest. "You haven't been happy with Jake for a while. This was a long time coming. I'm here if you need me."

"Thanks, Jules. I've learned my lesson. No more men. That's the last thing I need."

As STRESSED out as I have been all day preparing, everything has gone off without a hitch. I already touched base with Jules and Cameron and both reported things are going well. Everyone is happy and the desserts are a hit. I have to admit, I am feeling pretty good for the first time in a while. I am back in charge and taking care of business.

The Holly Hop has brought in an even larger crowd than usual. All the seniors are here, as well as many others from neighboring towns. All are dressed to the nines and on the dance floor. It is sweet to see so many old couples dancing together, holding each other tight. It is adorable, but also makes me feel the slightest bit jealous.

The dessert table is going great, and I have received so many compliments on my pies and pastries. I spent the last half hour walking around and talking to a few of my regulars from the bakery, and as I am walking back to the dessert station, I am greeted by Norma Andrews.

Norma comes in every month and orders a tray of cookies for her book club. She always challenges me with her unusual requests because she likes to match the food to a theme that goes along with the book. It is a fun challenge and gives me a lot of freedom to be creative. She is one of my favorite customers.

"Callie! Your delectable creations never fail me. I'm sad they're almost gone, though! Do you have any more you're hiding back there behind the table?"

"Almost gone?" Shocked, I walk over and see she is right. The table mostly picked over. The crowd has ravaged the food and there isn't much left. "Oh my goodness! I can't believe it went so fast!"

"It's all so delicious. I normally see people ordering dinner, but I think when everyone heard you were catering, they were happy to just stick to dessert. The red velvet bites are perfection!"

"Thank you so much! I better run back to the shop quick and grab a few more platters. I have some cookies and tartlets I made just in case! I'll be right back."

I knew I should have brought over the extras! Usually, popping over to the bakery would be quick, but with the crowds and the street being shut down, it is bound to take longer. The last thing I want is an empty dessert table.

I try calling Jules and there is no answer. She is probably knee deep in sugared up little kids and can't hear her phone. I don't bother to call Cameron; she can't leave the truck unattended. The only option is to run and grab it myself.

I rarely wear heels, so I try to be careful as I rush, zigzagging through the dance floor to get to the door. I am right at the doorway to leave when my foot slips in a puddle of slush that had been tracked inside. My feet slide out from under me and in one fell swoop I land hard on my back, slamming my head onto the unforgiving concrete and all goes dark.

I AWAKE in blazing pain and slowly flutter my eyes open. Kind, familiar blue eyes stare down at me, concerned and searching. I shake my head lightly, trying to snap to it.

"Don't move," Gabe says as he takes my hand gently in his. "Take it easy. Do you know where you are?"

Oh my goodness. I'm hallucinating.

I close my eyes and try to avoid focusing on the pain radiating from the back of my head. When I open them again, Gabe is still there. Above his head, mistletoe dangles in the entryway of the door, taunting me.

Callie - 0 Evil Mistletoe - 1

"Callie? Can you say something?" Gabe calls over his shoulder, this time louder, and to no one in particular. "Can someone call an ambulance? She's not responding."

"Wait, no. I'm fine. I'm just... Gabe? How... what... how are you here?"

He smiles down at me warmly, a flood of relief washing over his face. "You scared me for a minute there. You fell right as I was coming in and slammed your head pretty hard."

"I'm so confused." I say, looking around at the crowd that has gathered in a circle around me. Doris Winkleblack stands behind Gabe, looking worried.

Gabe continues his line of questioning. "Do you know where you are? What's your name?"

"Yes, I'm Callie Parker. I'm at Kielty's, but I should be getting more food for the dessert station instead of laying here in a freezing doorway causing a scene and blocking traffic," I say, growing more embarrassed by the minute.

He laughs heartily. "Noted. Mental faculties still in check."

I try to get up and Gabe eases me back. "Woah, woah, woah. Is anyone here a doctor? You shouldn't move. You could have a concussion."

I brush off his concern. "I'm fine. And you still haven't answered me. What are you doing here?"

He ignores my question, turning to look up at Doris and says, "I'm basically just copying everything I've seen on TV about concussions. Think she will be ok if she gets up?"

Doris pats Gabe's shoulder, no longer worried about me, and chuckles. "You're doing a great job." She looks back and forth between us, her eyes sparkling with interest, assessing the situation. "How do you two know each other?"

Now it is my turn to ignore a question. Doris knows everything about everyone. She almost gets giddy with excitement when she stumbles upon information other people might not know. I'm sure she is already jumping to her own conclusions about Gabe and I.

"I'm fine, honestly. My head hurts, but I'm ok. I need to hurry back to the bakery and grab a few more trays. I don't want to run out and we're already low." I touch my hand to the back of my head and pull it in front of me to check. No blood. I'm good.

I push myself up as Gabe reaches over to help me stand. I must have moved too fast because I instantly feel dizzy and slip back down again. I reach out and grab onto his arms in a panic, and he holds my waist to steady me.

He looks down at me and my breath catches. I feel his grip

tighten ever so slightly as we stand together, once again, neither of us saying a word.

Goodness. The way he looks at me.

I can't help but notice the feel of his strong biceps under my hands and how my heart quickens at the thrill of being close to him. In that instant, I am almost glad I had been a clumsy mess.

Doris is clearly picking up on the vibe and beams at us. "Did you two notice you're under the mistletoe? You know what that means, don't you?"

Subtle, Doris. Subtle.

Gabe snickers and I quickly let go of him and back up. He makes no qualms about showing he is disappointed.

Doris, however, is relentless and isn't about to give up. I know exactly what she is doing. She must have heard about Jake and is trying to play matchmaker. "Callie, you shouldn't be running around alone after a fall like that. Why don't you take Gabe over with you to your shop and he can help carry the trays?"

"No, I'll be right back. It will only take a few minutes. I told you, I'm ok." I smooth out my dress and realize I was about to run out of here without a coat. Gabe must have noticed at the same time.

"I'd be happy to help with the trays." Gabe offers his black wool coat to me. "Here, allow me. It's cold out there." He drapes his coat over my shoulders, grazing my arms as he assists, and his sexy lips curve into a smile. My stomach flips as if I were on a roller-coaster.

I mumble thanks as I rush out the door, not wanting to talk any more.

I am so screwed.

CHAPTER 8

GABE

I catch up to Callie in the street. "So the business you own is a bakery?"

She just stares at me and keeps going, stomping her way through the slush and snow down the street. If I didn't know better, I'd think she was angry with me. I press on anyhow.

"You know how many bad jokes I can make with that information? Let's see, something about you being a treat... sweet... no, about giving me a little sugar?"

She stops dead in her tracks and turns to face me. "What's going on? Did you hunt me down or something? Find out my name and follow me here?"

Surprised, I take a step back. "No, of course not. Why would you say that?"

"You show up here out of nowhere at an event I'm catering. Just seems a bit odd, don't you think? Hopemeadow isn't some big city."

"I told you why I came to Connecticut. The building my grandfather left me is in Hopemeadow."

Her mouth drops open in shock. "It is? Why didn't you tell me?"

"Are you kidding?" I laugh. "You said you didn't want to share details. You never told me where you lived. I'm just trying to follow your lead. I have nothing to hide. I'm just as surprised to see you here." I step towards her again, lowering my voice a little. "Although it is a pleasant surprise. More than pleasant. I thought I'd never see you again."

I reach out to grab her hand, and she pulls away. "Look, you're great, Gabe. You're attractive, kind, a fantastic kisser, and probably all the things a woman could ever want…"

"How are you making all these compliments sound like a bad thing?"

"But I can't do this right now." Callie turns and starts walking faster down the street. I trot after her until I catch up.

"Do what? I'm just helping you grab some food."

She puts her hands on her hips. "Then why do you keep looking at me like that?"

"Like what?"

"Like… like you want to eat me!"

I burst out laughing. "Excuse me?"

"That came out wrong. You know what I mean!"

She looks adorable standing there furious, swimming in my coat, her cheeks flushed, hazel eyes blazing.

"Like that! Stop looking at me like that!"

I laugh again and shake my head. "I don't know what you mean, but you have to admit this seems like fate. Us finding each other again…"

"It's not fate. I just about cracked my head open."

"Under mistletoe…"

"Will you stop! If you're going to help, fine. But promise you're not some creeper stalking me, and you're not here to hit on me."

"Cross my heart, scouts honor." I put my hand over my heart and try to look earnest.

She looks at me skeptically, shakes her head, and turns to

continue stomping off down the street. I follow behind, a wide smile stretching across my face.

WHEN WE ARRIVE at the bakery, Callie makes me wait outside while she grabs the food from the back. She barely spoke to me on the way over and is doing everything in her power to keep me at a distance.

It's clear her focus remains on making sure her event goes well, and until she does that, she isn't doing anything else. I admire her determination, but I don't understand why she is so upset with me.

The kiss at the airport wasn't one sided. She kissed me back with a fever that matched my own. Yes, I initiated it, but we were in that moment together, just like we were again under the mistletoe at Kielty's. The connection between us is undeniable. I know she feels it, too. She looks stunning in that red dress and heels, and it took all my restraint not to kiss her again when I saw her.

But tonight she seems guarded, and there is no denying she wants to push me away. Maybe all the coincidences are freaking her out, but my gut is telling me it is more than that.

It isn't long before we are back at Kielty's. Callie directs me where to put the trays and immediately goes to work rearranging her station.

"Can I help with anything?"

"No, I'm good. Thanks for helping me carry these back. I probably wouldn't have been able to do it in one trip on my own."

"Glad to help."

She glances around, looking a bit uncomfortable, like she doesn't know what to say.

"Well, thanks again. You should go enjoy the Hop. They

always end the night with a dollar dance with Santa to raise money for the local food pantry. It's hilarious."

"Callie, can I…"

Just as I am about to ask if I could buy her a drink, I am cut off by a sweetly meddling Doris Winkleblack.

"Ahh, looks like you two survived the trip! Were you able to see the fire truck parade on the way back? Has it started yet?"

"No, not yet, Doris. Everyone looks like they are having a great time and are lining up though," Callie says as she rearranges her dessert display.

"Oh, you must step out in a bit so you don't miss it!"

I try again. "So Callie…"

"Did you know Gabe is staying at Hillside?" Doris interrupts, smiling sweetly and looking back and forth between us.

"No, I didn't know that," Callie says, looking at me warily. "Hillside is a beautiful inn. I'm sure Doris will make your brief stay here very comfortable. I hear her breakfast in the morning is quite the spread."

Not giving me a chance to respond, Doris continues, seemingly determined not to let me get Callie to myself. "Callie, you're so kind. You know, you've outdone yourself this year. Truly, spectacular." She leans in conspiratorially. "Years ago, before we were graced with your talents, we used to order cookie platters from Ned over at Johnson's. Back then, your grandmother wasn't able to keep up with orders for events. Anyhow, you don't know what a favor you did for us when you finally decided to go beyond the truck and take over your grandmother's shop." She looks around and then lowers her voice to a whisper, wrinkling her nose in distaste. "Johnson's cookies were like hard little saucers."

"Go beyond the truck?" I ask, curious. "Did you own a food truck?"

Again, Doris answers for her. "Yes, Callie worked her way through college with her food truck. She used to set up and serve all these delicious muffins, cookies, and breakfast sandwiches. It quickly became a town staple. It was hard to see that truck and not stop and grab something."

Callie blushes and brushes it off. "Oh, I'm sure Johnson's wasn't bad, but I'm grateful to have expanded. I couldn't let Honey's close up. I think Grandma would have been heartbroken."

"Here's hoping we can keep Bon Bon's out of Hopemeadow," Doris says, giving me a disapproving side eye.

It is only then that I understand what Doris said at the inn.

Callie owns the bakery next door to my building.

Callie looks alarmed, eyebrows raised. "Wait, what? Why would Bon Bon's be in Hopemeadow? Their closest store is an hour from here."

"Oh, you don't know?" Doris wears a smug smile. "Gabe is selling Lou's old building to Bon Bon's. They want to put one of their bakeries right next door."

CHAPTER 9

CALLIE

Stunned, I stare at Gabe. "*That's the building you own? The one next door to my shop? And you're selling it to Bon Bon's?*"

Gabe shifts uneasily. "Nothing has been decided yet, but they have shown interest. They are coming to see it this week."

Just then I hear Hank's voice call out from the door, "Hey all! The parade is getting started!" A few people start grabbing their coats and head towards the door.

"Excuse me, I have a few things I need to attend to." I walk off, not waiting for a response.

I have to get away. My head is swirling. I disappear behind the bar and into the kitchen to escape. I am close with Don Kielty, the owner, so he won't have a problem with me hiding back here. He sees me as I make my way to a chair near the walk-in freezer, plop down, and put my head in my hands.

"Hey little darlin'! How's the Hop going? Everyone looks like they're having a great time."

I look up and give him a weak smile. "It's been quite the night, Don. How are you doing?"

Don has been a big supporter of mine over the years. He

has to be in his late 60s and every time I see him he looks a little more worn and tired, but happy. When I took over the bakery from my grandmother, so much was in disarray. She was the heart and soul of Honey's, but was not a business-woman. When I came in, I didn't know where to start. I had just graduated with a degree in business, but putting it into practice was a different story. Don took me under his wing and helped me get everything organized. He showed me how to keep track of the books and tipped me off on a few great vendors and contacts at local farms. He is like my small business fairy godfather.

"Can't complain," he says as he looks me over and furrows his brow. "I heard you took a dive and hit your head. You feeling ok? Have you eaten anything?"

"I'm fine. Just a rough night. A rough week, actually, and I'm struggling to keep it all together."

My eyes well up with tears. First Jake and now Bon Bon's might be coming. There's no way I can expand Honey's if Gabe sells the building and, even though the shop is doing great, I can't afford to buy it just yet. Everything is crashing in around me, and now Gabe is here. I feel more confused than ever.

Don walks out from behind the grill and crouches down in front of me.

"I'm not quite sure what's going on, but I do know this: sometimes you have to fall apart to figure out what pieces need to come back together and what needs to go in the trash." He reaches in his pocket, pulls out a packet of tissues, and hands me one. "Do you want to talk about it?"

I take the tissue and blot at my eyes. "I'll give you the short version. Looks like Lou's building next door is being sold, and possibly to Bon Bon's. I've been hoping to expand Honey's into that space and now if it sells, not only is that not possible, but Bon Bon's could put me out of business."

Don sighs. "I can see why that would make you upset. Have

you gotten in touch with the owner? Are they willing to sell to you instead?"

"I can't afford to buy the building right now, but I had been calling and trying to reach the realtor for a few weeks to see if they could put me in contact with the owner. I put together a proposal that outlined my renovation plans and would give the owner a partial stake in the business."

"They aren't answering you? Can you find out who the owner is and contact them directly?"

I take a deep breath and grumble, "I know who he is now."

"Great! Then go for it, Callie. Set up a meeting and get what's yours. Don't go down without a fight. You know as well as I do that Hopemeadow wants you here, not Bon Bon's. You have worked too hard to stop now. You've been talking about wanting to expand Honey's for years. Do whatever it takes and protect your business."

I sniff and look up at him. Don has never led me astray. "Do you really think I can do this? Am I trying to do too much? I might be in over my head, especially now that it looks like a regional franchise is coming after me. Why else would they want to buy the space next door?"

"Callie, I've watched you grow up right before my eyes. You've got this. I believe in you. Don't let them think they can make you crumble that easy."

"Thanks, Don. I don't know what I'd do without your help." I lean in and give him a hug. "Now I just have to convince the owner to hear me out. He seems set on selling."

"Use all of your advantages. You're smart. And let me know how I can help."

Don gets up and goes back to the grill. He has never been one to protect my ego. He tells me the hard truth, even when I don't want to hear it, so I know he wouldn't tell me to go for it if he thought it was a bad idea.

But how do I do this? My attraction to Gabe makes everything more complicated. I can't mix business with pleasure, and I certainly don't want him to pretend he's interested in taking a chance on my business because he's looking to get closer to me.

I pull myself together and go back out into the pub with a plan. Admittedly, not a well thought out plan, but a plan nonetheless.

I scan the room and see Gabe is still at the bar talking to a few locals. He seems so at ease with everyone. I'm always awkward around new people and here he is walking into a random bar in a small town where he knows no one and he fits right in, joking and smiling. I watch as he lifts his hand up to his neck and rubs slightly, turning his head closer to hear what Fritz, the town mechanic, is saying. Those hands. It is hard not to remember how they felt on my waist, how they sent jolts all over my body. And it was so thoughtful of him to offer me his coat. What a gentleman.

Stop it. No more of that. Keep it together, Callie.

Back to the plan. I'll convince Gabe to meet me tomorrow at the bakery so I can pitch him my proposal. I'll just set some boundaries, that's all. We will be purely platonic from here on out and, hopefully, once I pitch him my proposal, he can become my silent business partner. It will be a win-win. This could actually work out for the best.

As if he feels my eyes on him, he looks over and sees me staring at him. The corners of his mouth turn up into a slow grin and he winks.

We will be nothing more, no matter how much my stomach flips when he looks at me. I need him to respect me and my business. I can't let those deep blue eyes tempt me with this insane connection we seem to have. Or his tall, lean body, full lips, strong, hard...

I'm off to a terrible start.

I take a deep breath and walk over to the bar, grabbing my coat from the rack on the way through.

"Sorry about that, I just had to check on something. How's it going? I see you met Fritz!" I say a little too enthusiastically. Gabe looks at me and tilts his head as if to say, *what has gotten into you?*

"Did you know Gabe here is in the wine business out in California? I was telling him how nice it would be to have a great wine shop nearby."

"I didn't know you were such a wine aficionado, Fritz."

Fritz blusters a bit and takes a sip of his Bud Light. "Well, I don't know what you mean by aficia-tacos or whatever you call it. I'm no wine snob, but I think it would be great for Hopemeadow to get a little more foot traffic here, don't you? We need to bring in some more people and boost the economy."

"Actually, yes, I do. Expanding businesses here is exactly what I'd love to see more of. Hopemeadow is up and coming! So much potential here."

Fritz eyes me suspiciously and then shrugs. "I mean, we're pretty small, so it is what it is. We make do."

"Oh, don't be modest about our little town, Fritz! Hopemeadow is growing leaps and bounds each year." I turn to Gabe before Fritz can respond. "Would you like to step out and see some of the parade? Sounds like it just got started."

"I'd like that," Gabe says as he puts some money down on the bar and grabs his coat. "Nice to meet you, Fritz. Good luck with the Patriots this year."

"They don't need luck, they've got skill!" Fritz hollers to us on our way out. Gabe laughs and throws a wave over his shoulder.

A blast of cold winter air stikes us as we make our way through the crowd. Groups of onlookers line the street on both sides, and the familiar sound of "Jingle Bells" rings out from the speakers on one of the fire trucks. They honk the horns and intermittently blare the siren as they slowly roll down the street. The children call out excitedly to the firefighters, hoping they will continue throwing candy in their direction. Christmas lights adorn the firetrucks and are sparkling, casting colorful beams on the snow all around. We make our way to the edge of the street to get a closer look as the parade goes by.

"So, Fritz said you are in the wine business?"

"Yes, I'm a wine distributor. I grew up around my grandfather's vineyards and his wine shops. Wine is in my blood, I guess."

"Do you help with the family business, too?"

"Not anymore." His voice hitches. "I want to make my own way."

I nod, sensing there is more to that story, but don't prod. We have the same goal. I might have taken over my grandmother's shop, but I don't want the world to see me and the business as just a continuation of what she had already accomplished. I need to do this on my own.

He pauses and then adds, "That's why I'm selling the building. The investment opportunity I'm about to be involved in could lead to great things down the road. It's important to me to be successful without it being handed to me and this money will help make it happen."

This is going to be harder than I thought. The sale sounds like it is more than your everyday business transaction. It's personal, for both of us.

I am tempted to use this opening to talk about my business proposal, but I need more time to hone my pitch. I have one shot, and I can't ruin it by blurting things out on the side of the road during a parade.

"I understand," I say, nodding in agreement. "What a coincidence you're right next door, huh?"

He smiles at me. "Some might say it's fate."

"Gabe, are you really this much of a romantic? Do you believe in that, for real?"

He thinks for a moment and then says emphatically, "Yes.

Yes, I believe in fate. The universe has a way of conspiring for you and making things happen. We may try to rail against it, but I do believe in a bigger plan. Maybe our paths were meant to cross."

I look at him curiously. I don't think I have ever met a man so confident and unabashedly open. Having been hurt so many times before, I can't help but wonder if he has an angle, but he seems genuine.

It's baffling to me.

I shake my head, dismissing the idea. "I don't know why the universe would go to all that trouble."

As soon as the word trouble is out of my mouth, I am pelted in the forehead with a piece of candy thrown from a fire truck.

I stand there stunned and then burst out laughing. Gabe rubs his hand over his mouth, shaking, trying to hold it back, but the minute he sees me lose it, he starts howling with laughter, too.

"Well then. Heard you loud and clear, fate," I say, wiping the tears from my eyes.

After a few moments, we calm down and watch the parade slowly flow down the street. It feels good to stand in silence together, not feeling like we had to talk.

Everything is so beautiful. The snow is pristine on the trees, and the twinkling lights give everything a magical glow. All the people around us are smiling and happy, and I am grateful to be part of this tradition, enjoying this simple pleasure.

The parade has finally reached the end and the last fire truck with Santa is coming through. Everyone has their eyes glued to the parade, myself included, until I turn and see Gabe. He isn't watching the festivities like everyone else. He is staring at me with an intensity in his eyes that could not be disguised. He doesn't look away, but rather holds my gaze, strong. Something about this moment and every moment I have with him feels exciting and new, but also like I've known him for years. My heart races at the implications of this, and I'm not ready to think about what that might mean.

I quickly turn away and pretend to watch the parade while my mind works overtime, rehashing all the reasons this needs to stop.

1) I cannot fall for a stranger who's leaving soon and whose only mission here is a sale that will hurt my business.

2) I will not let another man sidetrack me from Honey's and going after what I want.

3) If it seems too good to be true, it is.

I HAVE to protect myself and keep a safe distance. Too much is on the line. I can't lose my focus.

Determined and willing myself to stay detached, I turn to him and say, "Gabe, would you like to get together tomorrow? Maybe meet me at the bakery around noon? I'd really like to talk a bit more."

He smiles at me warmly. "I'd really like that, Callie. It's a date."

My eyes grow wide at the word "date" but, for some reason, I don't correct him.

CHAPTER 10

GABE

I can smell the bakery from a block away. I walk down the street, growing more torn the closer I get. I feel pulled here and drawn to Callie, but the more I think about this, the more I realize how insane it all is. I plan on heading back home to California soon. Chasing after a woman who lives across the country makes me a glutton for punishment.

When Doris first mentioned the holiday festival, I agreed to go, but had considered backing out. Standing around in the freezing cold and watching a small town parade? That's the exact opposite of what I wanted to do. But Doris was so convinced I should go and felt it was imperative that I see the town on such a special night. She seemed so proud of the event that I gave in. I only intended on staying for a half hour and then planned on heading back to the inn.

But when I saw Callie? It was like a scene from a movie. I opened the door to Kielty's and there she was. It was as if she was all I could see, the one I haven't been able to get out of my head, making a beeline straight for me. I couldn't move. I was transfixed, watching her glide, her red dress accentuating the curves of her beautiful body. Her determined hazel eyes shining, and her fair skin a striking contrast against her soft dark curls.

Standing near her at Kielty's, all I could think about was reaching out and touching her. Feeling my hands in her hair, wrapping my arms around her waist. I wanted more. I wanted to be near her and I wanted her all to myself. I didn't want to talk to anyone else or watch a parade. I was there for Callie.

Even I have to admit, all the coincidences are unnerving. It seems like we were destined to meet, but it is all happening so fast. I just met her. We shared one kiss and a conversation, and somehow that is all it took to keep her perpetually on my mind. Everything about her entices me.

Yes, there are complications around the impending sale, but I plan to enjoy the little time we have together while I'm in town. I am looking forward to learning more about her and for us to go on a proper date. If spending time with her is anything like that kiss at the airport, I'll take every second I can get.

The bells on the door chime as I walk in. My eyes search and find Callie at the register chatting with a customer. She is smiling broadly, laughing at something the old man has said.

That laugh. I need to hear that sound again and again.

I don't want to interrupt, so I walk over to a small table off to the side to watch and wait. Within minutes, I know the bakery is Callie's happy place. She seems in the zone, smiling, focused, and radiating confidence.

It's incredibly sexy.

There is nothing like watching a strong woman in charge and owning it.

Honey's is more than I anticipated for such a small town. It is charming and stylish. The glass cases display both usual and unique selections, so there is something for everyone. Standard morning fare is alongside an assortment of pastries and artisan breads. The croissants, danishes, and scones not only look delicious, but polished, as if made by the hands of a classically trained chef. Ornately decorated cakes and pies line another glass case and have the same impeccable sense of design and artistry. I am impressed and my stomach growls in anticipation of trying some of it.

Callie finishes up with her customer and, as she is waving goodbye, spots me sitting off to the side. She smiles, wipes her hands on her apron, and walks over. The other night she looked incredible dressed up in her red dress. Today she looks just as good, if not better, in a simple pair of distressed jeans, a plain white v-neck t-shirt, and an apron embroidered with a honey pot and dipper.

"Hi there. I didn't see you come in." She smiles warmly, but I can sense distance in both her stance and voice. Something feels more formal, and I'm not sure why.

"I didn't want to interrupt while you were working. This place is great."

"Thank you," she blushes, clearly proud, and adds, "Can I get you anything? I have a few things I need to wrap up quickly."

"I'll have one of your favorites and a coffee."

She tilts her head, questioning. "One of my favorites?"

"Yes. You're the expert. Whatever you like the most is probably the best."

She laughs. "Ok, you got it. The coffee is self-serve, so you can grab a cup if you'd like and I'll be right back."

I walk over to the beverage bar that is against the far wall. There are four different types of coffee and an assortment of teas. I choose today's special, which is an Ethiopian coffee blend I have never heard of, but smells great. I pump a cup from the carafe and make my way back over to the seating area. It is small but cozy, with a counter and barstools which appear to all be taken by regulars. In fact, the whole place seems to be buzzing and has a steady stream of customers.

I sit at one of the wrought iron bistro tables and take a sip of my coffee just as Callie comes back with a plate that she places in front of me.

"My favorite. A chocolate croissant."

"Looks decadent. This coffee is great." She sits down, watching the door and everything around me. She seems distracted.

"It's one of the first things my grandmother taught me how to make in this bakery. She started this shop, and I took over about 10 years ago. I've retained a lot of the original essence, but have tried my best to make it into something that is uniquely mine, if that makes sense."

"Yes, I understand that completely." In fact, it strikes a little too close to home.

"I'm sure you do, which is why I'm excited you'll hear me out today." She folds her hands neatly in front of her.

"Hear you out?"

"I'm not sure if you're aware, but I have been trying to get in touch with you for weeks, well before we met at the airport."

Confused, I sit back in my seat and my eyes narrow. "What do you mean?"

"I have been eyeing Lou's space for years, but obviously wouldn't do anything to risk his antique business. When he decided to close, I realized this was my chance to expand Honey's without feeling like I was going after the life work of an old man. I've been calling your realtor to get in touch with you to pitch you my proposal. Once you hear me out, and see the details of my 5-year plan, I'd like you to consider becoming a silent partner."

I stare at her as I realize what is happening.

"Let me get this straight. This isn't a date?"

"I never said this was a date. I said I wanted to talk to you more. I didn't think it would be appropriate to talk business at the Hop. I would really like to show you what a great opportunity this would be for us both."

"So, to be clear, it's not a date and I'm here for a business pitch?"

"Well... yes."

I sigh and take a big bite of the croissant. The light crispy layers of the pastry and rich chocolate interior keep me busy for a moment while I avoid responding.

This is all a ploy. She doesn't want me, she wants the building.

She stares at me, waiting for me to say something. In business, I know it is best to wait someone out and let them talk first.

She looks uncomfortable and continues. "Look, I know things have been confusing since we met at the airport. Neither one of us thought we'd see each other again, so it felt ok to just indulge in the moment and let ourselves get carried away."

"Indulge in the moment?"

"Yes... with the... kiss." It comes out almost strained, like she doesn't want to say it aloud.

"What about the kiss?"

Frustrated, she says, "Why are you answering everything I say with a question and acting like you don't know what I mean?"

"Because I obviously don't know what you mean. You were right there with me, 'indulging' back. It wasn't a one-sided thing."

Flustered, she shakes her head. "I know I'm sending all sorts of mixed signals, but Honey's is everything to me. Were you aware that someone was calling you to discuss a business proposition related to the property?"

"Yes, but it wasn't something I wanted to entertain." I say curtly, crossing my arms. "You asked me here under false pretenses. You knew I thought it was a date. What are you doing? Using me to get to my building? Think you can lure me in by batting those pretty eyes at me and I'll just hand it to you?"

Her mouth gapes open in shock. "How dare you! I just didn't want to launch into a business proposal on the street. It's not my fault if you think every woman wants you and must be interested if she asks to talk to you. You called it a date, not me."

"And you didn't correct me."

"So now that your ego is bruised, you don't want to hear my pitch?"

"I didn't say that." I lean back in my seat and try to wipe all emotion from my face. "Go ahead."

She looks at me warily. "This isn't exactly how I wanted to lead into this."

"There isn't going to be a better time, so..."

"Fine. My plan is to scale the business, and that starts with adding space, which is why a renovation and expansion into your property is essential. Extra space will allow for additional commercial ovens, another walk-in cooler, and a new freezer which are all key for me to take on more business. I've been approached by local supermarkets and restaurants to wholesale some of my baked goods, but I haven't been able to do it with my current limitations. The expansion would allow for a much larger seating area, and a stage for local talent to perform. We'd finally be able to cater to a nighttime crowd in a way we never have before. We could bring in bands, host events on site, hold open mic nights. An expansion would also mean I could add more open air seating and a patio in the back, so it overlooks the valley. The possibilities are endless and you'll see the variety laid out for you in my proposal."

She walks over to the counter, grabs a thick manilla envelope, and places it in front of me. I open it up and flip through, giving it a cursory look.

"You don't know the first thing about me and, I can promise

you, I know nothing about running a bakery. Why would you want me as a partner?"

"Necessity. I can't afford to buy the building from you outright. At least not yet, but in the meantime, you would be a silent partner. I would foot the bill for the renovations of the space, pay rent, and you would get a portion of the profits until you decide to either sell me the building or you can choose to stay on and reap the benefits long term. It's a win-win."

"Your place looks great and I'm sure you will make it even more lucrative, but I'm not interested. I need cash flow right now for an investment. In this deal, from what I can quickly see from the numbers in your proposal, it will be at least a year or two before I make any substantial profit. I would be standing still."

She seems at a loss for what to say. "With great risk, comes great reward?"

I laugh. "Is that a quote from a superhero movie?"

"Ugh, no! Can you please just take some time, look over my proposal, and consider it?"

"I'm sorry, I can't and I don't want to lead you on. I'm all but guaranteed to make a killing on the sale if I go with Bon Bon's. For some reason, this is the only space they want and they are willing to pay a premium for it."

She laughs bitterly. "Yeah, I know why. Do you know anything about Bon Bon's? They are a regional bakery franchise. They've been a direct competitor of mine for years. If they open a shop directly next door, not only would that destroy any chance of growing my business, but it would cut into my profit margins so deeply that it could put me out of business. My customer service and products are worlds above Bon Bon's but I can't compete with their lower prices."

"This is going to sound cold, but what does that have to do with me, exactly?"

"It doesn't bother you that your sale of this property could destroy a small business? I've lived here my entire life, and I look after my grandmother. I can't leave Hopemeadow and start up somewhere else."

"When they approached me, I had no idea who they were or why they were interested in the space. This isn't anything against you. I have my own reasons for selling, as well. It wouldn't make sense for me to get involved in an investment in a small town like this that has no chance of substantial growth. I'm sorry for being harsh, but that's the truth. I'm moving forward with the sale."

Tears well up in her eyes, but she holds them back and stays strong. It's killing me to upset her like this, but I have to be honest. I have plans for my future, for proving myself worthy again. I don't want to be blindsided by another woman.

"Gabe, please. Just give me a chance to show you. Don't just dismiss it. Take your time and read through my proposal. Look at my business while you're here. Watch how it's run. You'll see the potential."

She pauses for a moment, looking distraught, and then her face lights up with hope. "In fact, let me show you this town personally. You will see for yourself that it is thriving. We might be small, but there is a lot of opportunity here and you will fall in love with it like I have. The bakery is integrated with all the holiday events in the next few weeks. I'll take you around town and you can see it for yourself."

"I wasn't planning on staying that long."

"I know... you mentioned your grandfather lived here? I'm sure you could use this time to find out more about his time here, too. Many of the older residents have lived their whole lives here, so I'm sure they could help you. I bet Doris Winkleblack would be a great person for you to start with. Please, just stay two weeks, even if it's just to find out more about your grandfather. But I promise you will want to invest in my business and this town once you learn more. You have to see it and be a part of it to know."

I look at her stricken face and hate knowing I am the one causing it, but this is business. "I don't want to give you false hope. I'm not going to change my mind."

"I understand."

"Do you? I don't want you to think I'm leading you on. I fully intend to sell the building to Bon Bon's."

"I know. Just stick around and let me show you Honey's and what Hopemeadow has to offer. Think of it as an extended vacation. I'll be your tour guide."

I look at her warily. "A tour guide who's trying to change my mind and emotionally manipulate me with possible information about my dead grandfather."

She winces. "Ok, that was low of me, but since you're so convinced you're selling, it shouldn't matter, right?"

"You're relentless."

"No, I'm confident you'll want in. I do have one rule though while you're here."

"I haven't even agreed yet, and now there are rules?"

"It must stay strictly professional between us. No more kissing."

I lean back and frown. "I'm not a fan of this rule. I liked the kissing. The kissing was great."

"You and I both know it's a terrible idea. And when you decide you do want to take me up on my offer, we will be business partners. You shouldn't mix business with pleasure."

I run my hand through my hair and sigh. "Please, don't get your hopes up."

She pins me with a no-nonsense look. "Ok, then let me put it this way. I have zero desire to kiss the man who has his heart set on following through with a sale that could ruin my life. Better?"

Shots fired, target hit.

"Callie..." I plead.

She lowers her voice and says quietly, "Honey's is my life. It's my passion. My reason for everything I do. I won't do anything to jeopardize it, and I need to know that any business decision you make is just that: a business decision. Not something you do... for any other reason."

I feel a kick of guilt when I look into her eyes and see her determination. I can't say no to her. I've been honest and upfront about my plans for moving forward with the sale. This is the least I can do for her.

"Ok," I say, simply.

"Ok??" She bites her lip and her eyebrows shoot up in excitement.

"Ok. I'll stay. I can work remotely. It would be nice to explore more of the town my grandfather loved so much. I had scheduled next week off work anyhow, so it shouldn't get in the way too much." Her face lights up like a Christmas tree. "But do not misunderstand me. I am going to sell. This is a business decision. I'm not trying to hurt you. It isn't personal."

Callie stands up from the table and proudly tilts her chin up. "Then I hope you're savvy enough to notice a smart business opportunity when it's presented to you."

I hold my tongue, smiling, and let that one slide. "So, what do you plan to show me while I'm here?"

"First, take some time and enjoy that croissant. I'll bring a few other confections for you to sample so you can get a sense of our quality. Feel free to grab another coffee on the house. I'd like to get started as soon as possible, but I'm busy tomorrow. Can we meet up the day after?"

"Yes, sounds good. Don't be upset if you see my realtor Abby showing the building this week. She has a few appointments scheduled and I intend to move ahead with those."

She nods solemnly. "I understand. Just don't sell until the two weeks are up, ok?"

"It will take time to show the property and field offers, so I'm fine with that."

Callie eyes me carefully, grabs a pen out of her apron, and writes her number on an order pad. "I'll text you with the details. Do we have a deal?"

"Deal."

CHAPTER 11

CALLIE

"It's time to spill it, girl. What happened with you and Jake?"

Jules has been not-so-patiently hounding me about this since I got back from Jamaica, and I have been dodging the conversation. In my breakdown over the news about Bon Bon's, I told her about my encounter with Gabe at the airport, but I still haven't gotten into the trip with Jake. I pretend not to hear her and focus on my painting instead.

We decided to have our girls' night at Painted Creations, a small craft studio in town that hosts DIY wood sign workshops. I may be creative in the kitchen, but not when I'm holding a paintbrush. My signs never come out quite right. Tonight, I decided to make a rustic Christmas countdown board that I hoped I wouldn't mess up too much so I can hang it up in the bakery.

It isn't looking good.

"Does this look right to you guys?" I hold up my board. Even from that angle, I can see the paint has started to bleed underneath.

Cameron chimes in with her usual blunt honesty. "You

screwed it up again. You need to dab at it and use less paint on your brush." Cameron leans over and smooths out her stencil to make sure there are no air bubbles. She is a pro at this and her signs always come out perfect. I watch her for a moment, trying to figure out where I had gone wrong, and am struck by her effortless beauty. Tonight she is in a simple off the shoulder Coldplay sweatshirt, skinny jeans, and black work boots. She is one of those women who is just naturally beautiful. Cameron rarely wears makeup and almost never gets dressed up. Her wavy blonde hair frames her face perfectly, and she has the kind of immaculate skin that makes you recall Neutrogena commercials. She is a gorgeous tomboy, and it makes her that much more attractive.

If I didn't already love her, I'd have to hate her.

"Ugh, yeah. I wonder if I'll be able to fix it." I bite my lip and go to work trying to scrape off some of the extra paint.

Cam barely looks up from her stencil as she says, "And no changing the subject. I want all the details on how you broke Jake's heart and left him there alone, crying in paradise."

We stare at her in amused shock. Jules says what we are both thinking.

"Dang Cam, you're vicious. Remind me never to get on your bad side."

Cameron shrugs nonchalantly. "He deserves everything he gets."

"Why do you hate him so much? Didn't you have a crush on him in high school?" Jules says suspiciously.

Cameron narrows her eyes to slits. "Hey, watch your filthy mouth. I was young, dumb, and impressed by abs back then."

"Oh, like you're immune to it now?" Jules teases. "You don't think he's hot? I think he's gotten better looking with age."

Cameron's cheeks turn pink. "Hey, this isn't about me! I'm not the one who goes on a romantic vacation, breaks up with someone, and then stalls on telling her friends about it."

She turns to stare at me, pointing and jerking her thumb in my direction.

"Ouch. I think I have tread marks on my back from being thrown under that bus," I say sarcastically.

"Just pulling us all back on track so we don't forget what's really important here. Now give us the scoop."

I sigh and put my paint brush down. "It just became painfully clear that we should have ended things a long time ago."

Jules pipes in. "But what made you leave in the middle of the trip? You wouldn't have left mid-trip unless something terrible happened."

"For starters, the whole trip was about what he wanted. It was all adventure excursions and packed with back-to-back activities. When he surprised me with the trip, he promised nothing but relaxation. It was exhausting trying to keep up."

"Oh, you poor baby. He takes you on a free trip to paradise and tried to make you have fun!" Cam pretends to blot her eyes with a paper towel, feigning tears, and snickers.

I laugh. "No, it was a complete sham! He sold me on it by saying he thought I was burnt out and needed a break, and then ran me ragged while we were there. We're just different people."

Jules eyes me, considering. "That's annoying. But you could have just sent him off by himself and laid on the beach with a book alone. You didn't have to abandon him there. That's pretty rough, Callie."

"Ok, well, what would you think if your boyfriend charged the whole surprise trip on your credit card and then you saw him about to hook up with another woman?"

"No!" Jules gasps in shock, putting her hand on her heart. "I can't believe he would do that to you!"

"Yeah, me either. That's why I left."

Surprisingly, it is Cam that says, "I never would have pegged Jake as the type to lie and cheat."

"My credit card statement proves otherwise."

Jules continues to rub a mahogany stain on her sign with a rag, then carefully wipes off the excess. "So what did he say when you confronted him?"

"I didn't say anything. I just left."

Jules' mouth gapes open. "Wait, you never asked him about any of it? Don't you want to know what happened?"

"I don't need him to tell me what happened. I saw it all with my own eyes. No explanation needed."

"Well, maybe there is one. This just doesn't sound like Jake."

Cam agrees. "You know I'm not one to defend Jake, but I have to say, this is way out of character, even for him."

My back straightens. "Hey! Whose side are you guys on, anyway?"

Jules throws up her hands. "Yours, always yours! I'm just surprised he would do that. We've known him our whole lives. He's made some mistakes in relationships and can be a bit self-centered, but this is awful."

I press my hands into my eyes and rub. "Needless to say, it's over. I'm over it. Onwards and upwards."

Liz, the waitress, comes back through and drops off a bottle of wine we ordered along with three plastic cups.

"Classy," Cameron says.

"Perfect for us. We are some classy broads," I say, joking and then mumble absently, "Men are the worst."

Jules agrees. "Seriously."

Cam fills our cups to the rim. "Here's to no more men!"

We cheer and take a sip.

Jules rubs her hands together and her eyes brighten as she says, "I don't know about that. Callie might already have a new guy on the horizon."

I pick up my paint brush again and pretend to be interested in my sign. "I do not. Yes, Gabe's mind-numbingly attractive, but he's the enemy."

"Ahh, the start of all the best romances," Cameron leans in eagerly. "Now this is the story I want to hear."

"There's nothing to report, guys. Gabe owns the building next door and is here to sell it. If he sells to Bon Bon's, I'm screwed. But more than anything, I want that space so we can expand Honey's. Imagine how great it would be to have a stage and enough room to hold events? We could really grow. I was thinking it could be a series of events called Honey's at Night. We could do open mic night, karaoke, bring in some acoustic music, or maybe even poetry readings."

Cam rolls her eyes. "Alright, you had me until the poetry readings. No one wants to hear that whiney stuff."

I laugh. "I'm just spitballing here. But you get the idea. It would be a whole new world with the extra space and ability to expand the kitchen. We could even add a bar, guys."

"And what do you plan on doing to get your hands on that building?" Cameron says, faking an exaggerated wink and suggestively licking her lips.

"You're ridiculous," I laugh. "And it's simple. I'm going to wow him with my proposal and knock him off his feet with good old fashioned business sense, that's how."

Cameron groans. "Well, if that's not the most boring plan I've ever heard."

Jules gives me a knowing look. "Callie is leaving out the best part of all this. She met him at the airport before she knew who he was and they... drumroll please... KISSED!"

Cameron gasps in disbelief. "NO!"

"YES!" Jules laughs and beats her hands on the table in excitement.

I bury my face in my hands, embarrassed.

"Ok, so let me get this straight. You break up with Jake, leave him across the world. Arrive at the airport and promptly meet a new hunka-hunka burnin' hotness and make out with him before you've even unpacked your bags?" Cameron shakes her head and looks at me with admiration. "Girl, I have a whole new level of respect for your ability to move on."

"Stop! I never thought I would see him again, and it just happened. I was feeling down and he made me feel better." Jules wiggles her eyebrows at me. "Not like *that*. Through our conversation. It was nice. But it doesn't matter now. I let my guard down, but I won't be doing that again. He basically told me he intends to screw me over and sell to Bon Bon's. I'm hoping I can change that and make him a business partner, but that's it."

"Mmm hmm. Ok. Whatever you need to tell yourself. I don't think I could stay platonic with a guy who looked like that." Jules takes another sip of her wine, pinky out to show she's classy with her plastic cup.

"If he was about to ruin your business? It wouldn't be as hard as you think," Cam chimes in.

Jules tilts her head, considering. "Good point. Who would knowingly let a big corporation bully a small business?"

My stomach turns at the thought. I could never compete with a franchise like Bon Bon's.

I have to stay focused. I can't mess this up. Gabe Montgomery, get ready to be knocked off your feet. When I'm done showing you all of Honey's potential, you will be the one begging me to invest.

CHAPTER 12

GABE

Even from down the street, I know it is her. I'd recognize that long chestnut hair and the sway of her hips anywhere. She is in a hurry, and carrying a large white box, which I assume is filled with some sort of mouthwatering treat from Honey's.

I'm not a man who typically seeks out desserts, but even I have to admit that everything she gave me to try at the bakery was incredible. Did she train under a master pastry chef during culinary school? I'm curious to find out more and why she stays here when she could make a name for herself elsewhere. She mentioned checking in on her grandmother, but is that is the only reason?

Letting her down and resisting her won't be easy. But I am looking forward to exploring the town and seeing if I can find someone who knew my grandfather. I watch her as she turns and disappears into what looks like a bookstore.

I can always use a new book. Might as well stop in and "accidentally" bump into her. I am curious about what she has in store for us tomorrow anyhow.

I walk in and Callie is at the front of the shop with two other women. All three turn at once to look at me when I enter.

"Callie, what a coincidence," I say, smiling.

"Is it though?" she says, eying me with a hand on her hip. "You seem to be everywhere I am these days."

"Lucky me." I smirk. "I'm exploring Hopemeadow today."

The dark-haired woman with Callie gives me a half-hearted wave as a hello and looks me over. "Ah, the infamous Gabe. I'm Jules."

My reputation precedes me. Based on the chilly reception, I figure Callie has told her about Bon Bon's. She's going to be a tough one to win over.

The woman behind the counter comes out with her hand extended and wearing a shy smile. "Hi, I'm Paige. I'm the owner here at The Book Nook."

"Hi Paige, I'm Gabe. Your store looks great." I shake her hand and scan the stacks of books, admiring. "I could spend hours in here."

She turns pink and shifts nervously. "I'd be happy to show you around and give you the grand tour before the writers' group starts."

"Writers group?"

"Yes, we host a young writers' group each week. Callie supplies the sugar fix."

"I was able to sample a variety of her pastries yesterday. Callie is quite talented." I look over at Callie and can tell she feels uneasy with the praise, just as she did when Doris was doling it out the other night at Kielty's. How can a woman so confident and skilled in her work still not be able to take a compliment?

"Oh, it's..." Just as she is about to brush it off, a tall blonde haired woman comes rushing in looking panicked. She looks familiar from Honey's.

"Callie, I'm a total flake! I didn't realize my last exam was today. I had it on the calendar for next week. I can't miss this or it would delay my certification."

"What? Cameron, no! I promised North View we would have three people to help serve today. They need the extra hands."

"I'm so sorry. You know I would be there if I could. They only offer this exam once a year, and it's the last one I need for my teaching certification. If I pass, all I have left is finishing my coursework." Cameron wrings her hands, looking distressed. "I haven't been studying or anything this week, so I really screwed this up all around."

I lean over to Paige. "Catch me up to speed. What's North View?"

Paige fills me in. "Every year they pick one day in December and volunteer to serve the residents at North View Inn, a homeless shelter in Hartford. The three of them always sign up together and they've been doing it for years."

Cameron starts apologizing again. "I'm sorry. I should have checked my calendar before agreeing to today. Outside of working at Honey's and grad school at night, you know I never have anything else going on! I just assumed I was free. I'm probably going to flunk it."

"No, you'll do great. This is important. I get it." Callie sighs. "I'm just going to have to find someone else. But who's going to be able to jump in at the last minute? Paige obviously can't and I don't want to let them down."

Jules perks up and turns to me. "What about you? You're just hanging out. Care to do a good deed today?"

Surprised, I shake my head. "No, not my scene."

Callie whips around and glares at me. "Not your scene? This isn't like going to a club. This is helping others in need."

"I'm all for helping people in need. I think it's great what you ladies are doing. I donate every year to our local shelters."

"But you can't give any of your time?"

"I'm usually pretty busy and I figure the money is just as useful."

"You're not busy right now," Jules challenges.

In truth, I have no issue helping at the shelter. I would gladly jump in, but I know being so close to Callie and working alongside her all day would be more temptation than I can handle. I don't need to make this harder than it already is.

I try to come up with a good excuse, but I'm floundering. "I have a bunch of conference calls I shouldn't miss…"

"Clearly more important than helping homeless people in need of a good meal," Callie says, dismissing me. "I knew you were all flash and no substance. Just another self-absorbed businessman."

My eyes narrow to slits. "If you really think that, you don't know me at all."

"Looks like I know all I need to." She turns to Jules. "Let's go, we should get there early, especially with one less person."

They start to leave, and I begrudgingly call out. "Fine. I'm in."

As I follow them out the door, I swear I see Callie suppressing a triumphant smile.

WE SPENT the afternoon serving the residents at North View. Callie kept her distance from me, but it was torture watching her. I was hoping today would show me a side of her I didn't like. I convinced myself that she must have bad qualities that would turn me off and make this easier.

But I was wrong. She is funny and humble. She is kind and unbelievably gorgeous. She does this thing where she laughs and throws her head back, and I feel it clear in my gut. Watching her pull her hair up into a ponytail just about did me in. I feel like I am some pathetic teenage boy mooning over the gorgeous cheerleader.

Snap out of it, Gabe. You only want her because you can't have her.

Or at least that's what I try to tell myself. Deep down, I know it is more than that. I just don't want to admit it.

She has been avoiding me most of the day, but every once in a while I catch her looking in my direction. It is hot in the kitchen and after hours of standing on our feet we are all getting tired. I watch her slip out the back door to get some air. Against my better judgement, I follow her.

I find her leaning against a brick wall, head back, eyes closed. Seeing her like this sends something stirring inside me that feels primitive. There is no denying it; I want her.

"Tired?" I watch her eyes flutter open as they slowly find their way to mine. Locking eyes with her is like a shot of whiskey that goes straight to my head.

"Yeah, it's been a long day. It was good, though. Thanks for stepping up."

"You're welcome." We stand there quiet for a moment until I take the leap. "Let me take you out tonight."

"I'm busy."

She's such a terrible liar.

"We could get to know each other better."

"Unless it's related to business, I'm not interested."

"You can stop the act." I walk over and put both of my arms on the brick wall behind her, caging her with my body. I lean in and murmur in her ear. "What does a guy have to do to change your mind?"

I can smell the sweetness of her skin, a combination of lavender and vanilla mixed with something uniquely Callie I can't pinpoint. Being this close to her, feeling the heat radiate off her body, and her breath warm on my skin is driving me mad.

She points her chin up and looks at me defiantly. "You're not my type." I see her body quiver slightly, and I know I'm not in this alone.

"We both know that's not true," I say, trailing a finger lightly down her arm. "We could really enjoy ourselves while I'm here, you know." I pause, letting the idea of us linger. "Want to have a little fun with me?" I lean in, dangerously close to her mouth, staring at her lips with desire.

For a moment, it seems like she is drawing closer until she ducks out from beneath my arms, breaking free. "No, thanks. You're not my idea of a good time."

She stalks off, back into the shelter, leaving me standing there alone.

Does she really dislike me that much?

I am about to sit on the cold concrete steps when I spot one of the residents watching me, snickering. He is an older man with a ragged gray beard, and he is shaking in laughter. He obviously witnessed the whole scene.

"I'll have a little fun with you," he says mockingly, as he licks his lips and blows me kisses.

I sigh. I deserve that.

He throws his head back, still laughing to himself. By the way he is acting, it is the funniest thing he has seen all year.

"Got any tips for me, old man?"

"Yeah, I have a few tips." He pats the ground beside him as if to say, sit down. I walk over and stand across from him. He is resting on a pile of bags that appear to be his belongings and is wearing layers of ripped up clothes and dirty coats. It is freezing outside and the thought of him being out here in the elements without proper attire just about breaks me.

"First, let's do a trade," he says.

"A trade?"

"That watch for my words of wisdom."

My eyebrows shoot up in surprise. "My Rolex? You think I'm going to give you my Rolex? How do I even know if your advice is worth it? Can't make a trade like that without a sample of the goods."

The old man claps his hands together and rubs them vigorously, as if he is about to launch into something big, and then hits me with some hard truth.

"First of all, she isn't the kind of woman who's just looking for a good time. That macho stuff won't win her over. I've known Callie for years through North View, and she's the best there is. She's not going to swoon because some pretty boy offered her a roll in the hay."

I smirk. "Is that so?"

"That's so."

"Alright, that's fair." I think for a moment. "What would make her swoon?"

"If you really want to win her over, there's only one way: the grand gesture."

"And what might that be?"

"It's different for every woman, but it has to be something that shows you are willing to put aside your own happiness for hers."

I nod my head and put out my hand. "I'm Gabe."

"Bennet."

We shake hands, and I hand him my watch. His smile grows wide as he puts it on his wrist, admiring it from different angles.

I turn to go back inside. "You're a smart man, Bennet. It was nice talking to you. Merry Christmas."

"Merry Christmas, Gabe." He salutes me and I head back into the kitchen. I get back in the line and start serving. We only have about a half hour left. Within a few minutes, Bennet is in line and getting lunch. He reaches Callie first.

"Hi Bennet! How have you been?" She serves him a plate of food, and I am reminded of just how many residents she seems to know on a first name basis.

"Just dandy. I've been thinking about going into the psychology field. I think I'd make a great therapist." He winks at me, dramatically checking the time on his new watch, and I shake my head, laughing.

He walks off as Callie stares at Bennet's wrist, noticing the watch. "I know that watch!" She walks over to me and lifts my left hand. "He has your watch!"

"Yes, he does. Good eye." To tease her, I lean in and whisper, "Have you been checking me out?"

She blusters. "No! Don't flatter yourself. I just remember it from the airport when I thought you were a thief. How did he end up with it?"

"We made a trade," I say simply.

Her jaw drops. "You traded with Bennet?? What did he give you?"

I shrug. "He's a good man. He's got a lot to offer."

Callie looks flustered, like she can't understand what happened, especially in the context of the guy she has pegged me to be. I try to change the subject.

"Jules, let me take over for you with the mashed potatoes. Go take a break. You've been working for a while."

Jules looks relieved and pats me on the back. "Hey, thanks Gabe. You're not so bad."

I grin at her. "You're not so bad, yourself."

"Enough of that! No becoming friends, you two!" Callie says, frustrated, throwing her hands up in the air.

Jules walks outside, and I turn to Callie. "We could be friends too, you know."

"You don't want to be just friends."

"True, but I'll settle for what I can get. I've enjoyed working with you today. You've got a good heart. You focus on what matters. I respect that. Can't have too many friends, right?"

Her eyes twinkle, and she cocks her head to the side, considering. "That's quite the turn around from five minutes ago."

I laugh. "Woman, cut me some slack. You can't blame a guy for trying. Trust me, I get it now. You're not interested. I struck out. I surrender."

She smiles. "Ok. Well, in that case I'd like to be friends."

I stick my hand out. "Friends."

We shake hands and instantly the air between us feels charged. It's electric. It is like this every time we touch. Scratch that, it's like this every time we are even in the same room.

The word "friends" hangs in the air and neither of us says anything for a moment, still holding each other's hand. Her mouth parts, as if she is about to say something, and she leans in slightly.

"Hey!" A woman calls out to me from the line. "Yeah, you, the poor man's Clooney. Can I get some lunch or what?"

Callie giggles. "Better get to work, Clooney."

I give Callie a sheepish grin and salute the woman in line. "Yes, ma'am. Coming right up." I continue serving and am lost in thought, contemplating grand gestures.

Friends. For now.

CALLIE

"WHEN IS MR. HOTTY-WITH-A-BODY SHOWING UP?" JULES ASKS from inside the truck.

I burst out laughing. "Jules! You're killing me! Enough with all that already. We've officially decided to try to be friends and seeing him in action yesterday makes me think he would be a great silent partner for Honey's. I'm not sure what happened with Bennet, but he came back and made a point of telling me Gabe is a good guy."

"Of course he thinks that. He gave him his ridiculously expensive watch."

I shrug. "He didn't have to do that. It was generous of him."

"True, but why is he still planning on selling to Bon Bon's? You told him they were trying to run you out, right? That would break you."

"He has his reasons, I'm sure. But I know that once he sees Honey's and gets to know Hopemeadow, he won't do it. And it's not just Bon Bon's. I don't want him selling to anyone except for me. I just need time, that's all."

Jules looks hopeful. "Maybe going into business with him was meant to be. All of these coincidences are a little weird."

I don't have an answer to that. Gabe seemed convinced at the Holly Hop that it is fate and who knows? Maybe it is. Maybe I was destined to meet him so I can expand Honey's and continue my grandmother's legacy. But I keep going back to the kiss, the shock of seeing him again at Kielty's, and the way he makes me feel.

I hand Jules the money for the cash box in the truck. She clears her throat and says, "So, not that you seem interested, but Jake called again this morning. He sounded mad."

"You're right. I'm not interested."

"He said he was back in town."

I shift nervously, but keep a brave face. "It doesn't matter. It's over."

From a distance, I see Gabe getting out of his rental car and start walking over to us. I feel a wave of heat spread through my body. I keep myself turned towards Jules so it isn't so obvious I am watching him out of the corner of my eye. The last thing I need is for him to realize the fireworks he sets off inside me every time he is around.

"He might be a jerk for wanting to sell, but dang, that man is freaking gorgeous." Jules pretends to fan herself with a stack of napkins.

I swat at her and hiss, "Stop it! He might hear you."

Jules laughs. "He's like 20 feet away." She whistles lightly. "Girl, he is staring at you hard. Why can't anyone look at me like that?"

Even from a distance, when he looks at me, it's like there's no one else around. It's unsettling in the best way. He is dressed down in jeans today and still has that five o'clock shadow that accentuates his jawline.

Must stay platonic. Think about business. Anything but those lips.

"Hey there. Welcome to the Hopemeadow Ice Rink!" I say a bit too enthusiastically.

He grins at me. "Hey you." He takes a moment and looks around. "This place looks like it could be in a Hallmark movie."

I have to agree; the outdoor ice rink is idyllic. We got a dusting of snow last night, so everything looks fresh and new around us. The zamboni just came through and cleaned the ice, and the sound of skates gliding and scraping across the rink mingles with kids' squeals of excitement. Open skate has started and it is a gorgeous sunny day. I feel hopeful that this is a great introduction to Hopemeadow and shows off one of the additional sources of revenue for the bakery.

"Adorable, right? This afternoon is free skate but they also do lessons and leagues here throughout the winter." I turn to Jules. "You remember Jules. I don't know if you're aware, but she's my right-hand woman at the bakery. Those incredible artisan breads and biscotti you saw at the shop? That's all her. She also mans Honey's Treat Truck here during open skate on the weekends. We provide all the concessions."

"Nice to see you again, Jules," Gabe smiles and Jules blushes.

"Nice to see you," she purrs back.

I shoot her a look that threatens, *don't you dare,* and Jules shrugs at me with a smirk.

Just then Gabe's cell phone rings. He looks down to see who it is and says, "Sorry, this should only take a minute."

He steps off to the side to take the call and Jules mouths to me in a barely audible whisper, "He's so hot." I stifle a laugh and shake my head at her.

She's not lying. The back of him is just as nice as the front.

I hear Gabe's voice grow tight. "What do you mean they were scared off? What happened?" He turns in my direction, giving me a stern look.

What did I do now?

"I'm sorry, Abby. I can't believe that happened. It's possible some in the community got wind that Bon Bon's has shown interest in the property and thought they were the ones visiting today. Thanks for letting me know. Keep me posted on what they say and if they'd like to reschedule... ok, thanks, bye."

Gabe puts his phone in his pocket and walks over with an irritated expression on his face.

"What are you trying to do, Callie?" I haven't seen him angry before. I don't like it, especially when it is directed at me.

"Excuse me? I'm not sure what you mean."

"You know what I mean. My realtor just called me."

"And how does that involve me?"

"She told me what happened at the showing this morning." His jaw clenches as he crosses his arms. "Tell me the truth; did you ask me here as a ploy to make sure I wasn't there when it all went down?"

"When all what went down? You're starting to freak me out. Honestly, I have no idea what you're talking about."

"Abby said when she arrived with the potential buyers, five people were in front of the property picketing."

"Picketing?? About what?"

"They had signs that said 'Heck No, Bon Bon's has to go' and were chanting it. They circled them as they were in the front."

I gasp and quickly cover my hand over my mouth to conceal a laugh.

He stares at me, annoyed, head tilted. "Callie, I thought we had a deal."

I raise my hand as if taking an oath. "I swear, I had nothing to do with it."

"How would anyone even know that I had showings today?"

I can feel my cheeks redden. "I might have mentioned it to Doris when she came in to pick up her weekly order for knitting club, but only because I'm concerned, not because I thought anything like that would happen! She must have told people."

"Obviously," he mutters. "She said the potential buyers, who were not with Bon Bon's by the way, were so shaken by the whole thing that they didn't stay to view the building. They said they would come back another day 'when things settle down.'"

"I'm sorry, Gabe. Truly. That's not anything I would condone, and I can promise you I wasn't involved in that." I pause for a moment and without thinking add, "It is nice to know that people want me here and want to protect me, though."

"I'm not out to get you, Callie." He seems angry again.

"I didn't say you were, but you have to admit it's nice people would go to all that trouble."

"Maybe so, but you need to call them off. We had a deal that I would continue showing the property."

"You're right. I'll talk to her and see if I can find out who was behind it."

"I'd appreciate that." I can tell he is trying to continue staying mad at me, so I jog up into the truck and come back with a small white bag.

"One of the best sellers from Honey's Treat Truck is our giant chocolate chip cookies." I smile and extend it out to him as a peace offering. "Cookies make everything better."

"First the croissant and now this? You can't always feed me to make things better."

I chuckle and nod in agreement. "I don't plan on making you mad often, so just take the cookie."

He accepts the cookie and his face softens. He walks over and stands next to me so we are side by side, looking out at the ice skating rink together. "Ok, I can see why you brought me here. Looks like it's a great opportunity for Honey's, but just so you know, I can't ice skate. I'm a California guy, remember?"

"Lucky for you, I didn't plan on us ice skating today."

He looks relieved. "Oh, then what's the plan?"

"The rink has a special visitor today."

"Is that why there are so many cars and a line of people over there? Is it Santa?" he asks as he dives into the cookie bag.

"Way better than Santa," I say with a sly smile.

WE WALK BACK into the facilities building and past a line that is forming. Kids in snow pants, bound up in scarves, are squirming and not so patiently waiting for their turn.

"Now I'm intrigued. This isn't a line to meet Santa?" Gabe peers around me to see past to the front.

I laugh and guide him to the front of the line where there are a few elves helping guide the children. Just ahead is an area decorated like the North Pole, with snow-covered trees, gingerbread houses, and candy canes. Two large faux wooden doors are in the center. One of the elves presses a large red button to open the doors as a child comes out licking a candy cane and holding a package of peppermint bark.

"Hi guys!" I say to the elves. "This is my friend, Gabe. He's here to meet Peppermint."

"Hey Callie. Sure, anything for *you*," Nate says as he glares at Gabe.

The two Christmas elves, Jimmy and Nate, are teens I know well from the bakery. It is hilarious seeing them in tights and elf shoes, and I make a mental note to get a photo with them at some point this season to put up on my bulletin board at the shop. They come in regularly after school with a few of their friends. They are sweet kids, but I don't understand the hostility towards Gabe.

"Nice to meet you fine elves," Gabe says, extending his arm out to shake hands. They don't reciprocate and instead continue to stare him down. Gabe puts his hand down, leans in towards me, and whispers, "It's a bit chilly here in the North Pole, eh?"

I chuckle and pull him off to the side so we can wait to be let in.

"Ok," Gabe says while looking around and taking in the crowd. "I'll bite. Who's Peppermint?"

"Peppermint the Penguin is the star of Hopemeadow's annual Christmas play," I say matter-of-factly.

"We're here to visit a penguin?" He groans and rolls his eyes.

"Not just any penguin. Peppermint is a tap-dancing penguin who lost the holiday spirit and can no longer do his signature Christmas shuffle. His popularity has grown over the years and kids come out in droves to visit him."

"The kids come to cheer up a depressed penguin?"

I laugh. "No! You'd have to see the play, but basically, he takes a journey to visit each of his friends in the North Pole to see if they can help him find his shuffle. But when he arrives at each of their homes, he ends up helping them with a problem they are having instead."

"Ahh, ok, I see where this is going."

"It's a great message for the kids. By the end of the play, Peppermint finds his shuffle and learns the holiday spirit is alive and well within him, especially when he is giving and helps others. Families loved it so much that they started asking if he could make appearances at different holiday events."

"It's a great concept. Less materialistic, for sure."

"Yes, and the in-person appearances are similar to how kids sit with Santa, but instead of telling him something they want, Peppermint asks each kid what they can do to keep the holiday spirit alive and how they can help others. When the kid shares their idea, Peppermint tells them he will try it too, so he doesn't lose his shuffle again. Each kid walks away with a candy cane and peppermint bark as a gift, so there's still a touch of bribery involved."

Gabe laughs. "And that's where you come in."

I smirk. "Yes. I recently signed a contract with the town to provide all the peppermint bark he distributes. It's perfect because I can make it in advance of the season and Jules is already here to deliver it each week when she mans the treat truck. It's been a tremendous boost to Honey's."

"Smart. There are a ton of kids here."

"Yes, and I brand each of the bags, so it's good advertising, too. A lot of families travel here from nearby towns. I've had quite a few customers come in to Honey's and say they heard about it through this event."

"You're pretty clever, Callie." He stares at me with admiration in his eyes. I don't know what to say. I'm not used to someone being impressed by my business strategy. Jake never seemed too interested in any of it.

Jimmy the elf presses an oversized red button, and the doors swing open with a dramatic puff of smoke. They're getting fancy this year with the effects.

We walk through the doors and there is Peppermint the Penguin, sitting on his throne, awaiting his next visitor. He looks adorable in his usual full tuxedo, tap shoes, and a bowtie made of holly.

This year Peppermint is being played by Jed who works at the gas station in town. At least I am pretty sure that is Jed in the giant, oversized penguin suit.

"Hi Peppermint! How's it going?"

Peppermint waves his arms in the air above him. "Well, if it isn't my favorite sugar pusher. To what do I owe the honor?"

"I wanted my friend Gabe to meet you and see this Hope-meadow tradition in action. Gabe, this is Peppermint, also known as Jed when not in disguise."

"Gabe?" Jed's voice has an edge to it as he stands up. "Is this the jerk who's trying to run you out of business?"

"He's not trying to run me out of business. He does own Lou's old building and is considering selling. I'm hopeful I can convince him not to sell though once he sees everything

Honey's and Hopemeadow has to offer from an investment perspective." I wink at Gabe and shoot a smile over at Jed, trying to show him everything is fine and to keep the peace.

Jed waddles over, unable to move fast in his costume, and gets in Gabe's face. "Callie is like a sister to me. You should be ashamed of yourself putting her business in jeopardy like this."

Gabe looks surprised at the confrontation, but smirks. "I think you misunderstand the situation. Honey's is great and I respect all Callie has built here, but it's hard to take you seriously right now, Peppermint."

"You better take me seriously," Jed says a bit louder, although muffled through the penguin costume. "Do you know how hard she works and how much she gives back? Do you even care? Or are you one of those selfish pricks who only thinks about himself?"

Jed gets closer and bumps him with his belly. Gabe laughs and shakes his head in disbelief. "You're making a lot of assumptions about someone you just met. Why don't you shuffle on over back to your seat and calm down. Callie doesn't need you to protect her."

For as long as I've known Jed, he's always had a bit of a temper. But he's a great friend and loyal to a fault. Growing up, I witnessed him get in one too many fights defending others, and I do not want that happening here, especially with Gabe.

I place a hand on Jed's shoulder. "Hey, take it easy. Everything's ok."

"It's not ok. What I'm seeing is a guy who is nonchalant about the fact that he could ruin someone's life and has the nerve to let her spend her days showing him around town, begging him not to."

Jed doesn't wait for a response. He takes a step back and uses all his force to push Gabe. Gabe is caught off guard and falls stumbling backwards, tripping over a decorative candy cane, twisting, and lands face first on the edge of a gingerbread house display.

"Jed!" I yell as I run over to check on Gabe. "That's enough! What's wrong with you?"

"Callie, don't let this guy fool you. We've all got your back." I jump up and get in his face, ripping the head of his costume off so I can look him in the eye.

"I don't need anyone to have my back," I seethe. "Gabe is not the bad guy here, ok? Now everyone needs to leave him alone or they are going to have a real problem with me, do you understand?"

Jed looks shocked and then instantly full of regret. "I'm sorry, Callie. I just don't want anyone to hurt you. We all care about you."

My voice softens. "I know and it's very sweet, but this stuff has to stop."

Jed picks up his penguin head and waddles over to Gabe, extending his hand to help him up. "Sorry, man. I was out of line."

Gabe takes his hand and gets up, brushing off the bits of gingerbread display that are still embedded in his coat from the fall. "It's alright. Honey's is special. I'm starting to see why everyone is so protective of it." He looks directly at me while he is talking and makes my stomach drop. I'm not so sure he is talking about my shop anymore. "I get why everyone loves it so much."

I blush and come back over to Gabe. "I'm so sorry about all of this. Let's go out to the truck. I have a first aid kit out there."

"I'm fine."

"Well, you're bleeding." I reach over and gently touch his cheekbone that now has a small gash. He takes a sharp breath between his teeth and recoils a bit.

"I'll be ok, but I do think I should get going. I don't think I'm welcome right now."

We walk out from behind the faux wooden doors and off to the side exit where people are talking in hushed tones. They obviously heard the altercation and are lingering to see if they can figure out what happened.

We walk back to the truck and sit on the steps, side by side. I use an alcohol swab on his face and blow lightly on the cut. Gabe just watches me silently, eyes on mine.

"I'm really not trying to hurt you or anyone in Hopemeadow."

"I know that. I really do."

"I just want you to know that I do care what happens here. If it means that much to you, I won't sell to Bon Bon's, but I still need to sell the property. Just as it's important to you to keep your business going, I need that money to make an investment in my future."

"If you don't mind me asking, what exactly are you hoping to do with the money? Why is it so important to you?" I pause and then quickly add, "I know that's super invasive, so if you don't want to tell me, I understand."

Gabe sighs. "No, it's ok. It's a long story though."

"I'm not in a rush."

"Right after my grandfather left Hopemeadow, he took a chance on investing in a run down vineyard with one of his buddies out in California. Five years later, his friend didn't want to do it anymore and my grandfather bought him out. He made it his life and worked hard. D. Montgomery's became one of the premiere vineyards on the coast, and I grew up watching him create an incredible legacy. He scaled the business and added wine shops in different parts of the state. I always assumed part of the business would be left to me to run. I worked there, in various capacities, my whole life."

"So what happened?"

"I made a lot of mistakes when I was younger and took my family for granted. I stopped trying to prove myself and just assumed it would be handed to me, so I made a lot of bad choices. I was entitled. I played a little too much and let my family down. They paid my way through college and I coasted. It's hard to admit this or even hear myself saying it out loud."

I can hear the pain in his voice. "Everyone makes mistakes when they're young. It's how we learn."

"I just took it a bit too far. I stopped being reliable. My grades slipped. I didn't work and stopped coming around the vineyard and the shop, except for when I wanted to impress a girl. I gambled away family money. I traveled and didn't think twice about who I was hurting with my selfish behavior. My grandfather got upset and said I was being careless. We had a big falling out, and I was away when he died. In his will he left me this building and left the vineyard and all the shops to my mother. He wanted his legacy to carry on, and he wasn't sure if I could do that."

I reach out and grab his hand. "I'm so sorry, Gabe. That must have been hurtful."

"I deserved it. I wasn't ready to take all of that on back then, and that motivated me to get my life together. I knew I had to prove that I am someone who can work hard and be trusted." He takes a deep breath and rubs his neck with his hand. "So, that's the very long winded way of saying I'm working towards becoming a man that would make him proud. I know my mother would help me, but I want to do all of this on my own dime. I found an opportunity to invest in a small, up-and-coming vineyard that I think could go places under the right management."

"I can see why this means so much to you."

We stare at each other for a moment. It feels like we are two of the same, both trying to protect our businesses, prove ourselves worthy, and make our own way.

I look down at our hands intertwined and back up into his incredible blue eyes. They rage with passion and match what I feel inside. My heart races as he leans in, drawing closer, about to kiss me.

"Is this the reason you're not returning my calls?"

I swing around and there is Jake, staring at us together, teeth clenched.

CHAPTER 14

CALLIE

"Jake, what are you doing here?" I pull my hand back from Gabe's.

"You disappeared on me. What did you expect me to do?" he says, crossing his arms. He shoots Gabe a deadly look.

Gabe glares back at him, but stands up. "Maybe I should go so you two can have a moment alone."

"Good idea," Jake says, sneering.

"Gabe, just wait a minute. You don't have to go." I turn and look at Jake, fuming.

"I'll wait over here. This sounds like it's none of my business," he says and starts walking towards the parking lot.

I spin around towards Jake, simmering with anger. "You have no right to hunt me down. If I wanted to talk to you, you would have heard from me. You need to leave."

"Callie, you can't just cut me off like this," Jake says, changing his tone and pleading. "We have to talk."

"I can't get into this now."

"Then meet me tomorrow afternoon. I can come to you."

I look uneasily in Gabe's direction; he is almost to his car. I don't want him to leave without getting a chance to explain.

"Fine. Come during lunch," I say, defeated.

"Great. I'll see you then." Jake backs away reluctantly, watching me head off in Gabe's direction.

I run and catch up to Gabe. "I'm so sorry about that."

He shifts uncomfortably, a line etched between his brows. "What is there to be sorry about? I didn't realize you were involved."

"I'm not… well, not really. It's a long story. He shouldn't have come here."

He takes a beat before he says, "It's ok, you don't owe me an explanation."

Irritated, I step back. "I know that. I just didn't want you to get the wrong idea about things."

He crosses his arms. "What idea should I have?"

"He's not my boyfriend."

Gabe's lips curve into a smile. "Oh. Well, I'm glad to hear it."

I backtrack. "Not that you care or anything, since we're just friends and all. I just didn't want you to think I was keeping things from you."

"Noted." He steps in a little closer. "Well, this was certainly an eventful day."

"How's your face feeling? You ok?"

"Well, my ego is pretty bruised from being accosted by a giant Christmas penguin, but physically I'm fine."

I laugh. "It brings new meaning to 'Deck the Halls', am I right?"

Gabe's eyes grow wide with amusement. "Callie, was that a *joke*? I think that's the first joke I've heard you tell."

I feel myself growing red. I'm such a dork. "Stop it. I'm just messing around."

"That was possibly the worst joke I've ever heard." The side of his mouth quirks upward as he mocks me.

I punch him in the arm playfully. "Careful, bub. You've

already been beaten up by a penguin today. Don't make me be the next in line."

He laughs and throws up his hands protectively. "I admit defeat! Don't hurt me!"

I pull my coat tight and shiver. "I really appreciate you coming here today and seeing what we have going on."

"It's all great. You've cinched some great events around town. This truck is brilliant and a smart expansion of your business. I can't believe the line that has formed since we've been sitting here. Everyone loves it."

"Thanks, Gabe." I pause, searching for the right words. "I know where you're coming from about wanting to prove yourself and create something you can be proud of. I really do."

He gives me a small smile and says, "So, what's next on the agenda?"

"There's a fun event tomorrow night right on Main Street if you're up for it. The town choir leads a singalong with Christmas carols by candlelight in front of the tree at Johnson's grocery store at 6 p.m. Honey's will be there, of course."

"Hmm… that depends," he says reluctantly.

"On what?"

"Will there be any more of those chocolate chip cookies? If so, I'm in."

I laugh and nod. "I'll make sure to have some there just for you."

"Then I'll see you there." He smiles and turns to walk towards his car. Within a minute, I hear him cry out and turn to see him being pelted with a series of snowballs. Off to the side of a truck is a group of young boys, doubled over laughing.

"That's what you get!" One of them yells and couples it with an inappropriate gesture. Gabe makes a start as if he is going to go after them and they all shoot off like a bolt, running in opposite directions.

He looks at me again sheepishly, and I shrug, mouthing, "Sorry!"

HOPEMEADOW IS like many other small towns: everyone knows everyone, and that means everyone knows your business. The information about Gabe and Bon Bon's must have spread like wildfire, and I feel awful for what happened to him.

I made a few phone calls first thing in the morning to make sure people will leave Gabe alone. My first call is to Doris. She is the link to the town gossip chain, and I know if I have her ear it will make its way around just as quickly.

I told her what happened at the ice rink and how upset I am over how Gabe has been treated. I also made sure to mention that he promised he wouldn't sell to Bon Bon's. Doris seemed relieved to hear it and almost sounded a bit too satisfied, as if she had been the one to make him change his mind.

I wouldn't admit it to her, but it does give me a warm feeling knowing so many people are pulling for me to succeed. That is one of the main reasons I love it here: the people in this town feel like family. We look out for each other in our own way; sometimes it is misguided, but hey, we try.

It is almost noon, and I have been working since 4 a.m. My feet are killing me from running around all week, but I put it out of my head. Baking is like a form of meditation. Once I am in the zone, I forget everything else that is going on around me.

But today, even in my favorite place, I can't focus. I am a ball of nerves. I feel so unsure of everything that is happening in my life. I don't know how to deal with my conversation with Jake today. I don't know what is going to happen with Honey's and if I'll be able to take this place to the next level.

But more than anything, I feel myself falling for Gabe, and I know that is the most dangerous of them all. I haven't asked when Gabe is leaving, but I know it is soon. In fact, I haven't even asked if he has been over to visit his building next door yet. I have been so wrapped up in my own concerns that up until yesterday, I forgot that he has his own reasons here, too. I have been selfish. But falling for him would just be foolish. He will fly back to California soon to move forward in his life and here I will stay, unable to grow my business, and with a broken heart.

To make matters worse, Jake will be here anytime now. There is no doubt in my mind that it is over between us, but dealing with conflict is hard for me sometimes, especially in relationships. I tend to avoid the big dramatic scenes as much as possible, and it feels like Jake is pushing for one.

I just finished decorating cupcakes for a holiday party when I hear the door chimes ring. I look out from the window in the back and see Jake at the counter. He looks good. He always looks good. But now I see through all his charm.

I shouldn't put all the blame on him, though. I knew we had been on the wrong track for a while. I should have ended it months ago, but there is no excuse for what happened in Jamaica. The only reason I even agreed to this conversation is because I didn't want it happening in front of Gabe. It is embarrassing enough that Jake showed up at the rink, but I don't want Gabe knowing all the humiliating details of my failed relationship.

I wipe my hands on my apron, take a deep breath, and head out to the front. Cameron is working the counter, so I don't want to leave them together for too long. She has never liked Jake and has no problem letting him know just how little she thinks of him every chance she gets.

Jake flashes a hesitant smile when he sees me. "Callie. You look beautiful."

I look down at my icing stained flannel shirt, flour covered leggings, and blow my hair out of my eyes.

Could he be more full of it?

Cameron, who is grinding coffee beans and prepping coffee for the afternoon, starts the grinder the minute he begins talking to drown him out.

"Hi Cameron. Good to see you," Jake says a bit louder over the whirr.

Apparently, he is going to play nice with her today.

"Oh, you're here again. I thought we were done with you?" Cameron glares at him with an undisguised look of revulsion.

Jake's eyes flare with anger. "I see you're still a ray of sunshine. Maybe if you could convince someone to actually want to date you, you wouldn't feel the need to meddle in other people's relationships."

Ok, maybe not.

Cameron laughs and in baby talk says, "Aww, are you lashing out because you're super duper sad Callie has finally realized what a jerk you are? Here, let me get you a tissue."

"Enough you two," I say, feeling like I am refereeing two toddlers. "Cameron, let me know if it gets crazy out here and I'll hop back in. This should only take a couple minutes."

I turn to Jake and curtly say, "I don't have a lot of time, so let's make this quick. We should go into the back office for some privacy."

And to put some space between these two.

Cameron shakes her head as Jake nods and follows me into the back.

My office is small, with just enough space for a desk, a few filing cabinets, and two chairs along the wall. I sit in the chair behind my desk so he has to sit across from me, forcing space between us. I want to keep things formal.

He reluctantly sits down but inches the chair closer to the side of the desk.

"You can stay right there," I say. "What is it you want, Jake?"

"What do you think I want? I want to know what happened.

You just up and left me in Jamaica without a word. You don't think you owe me an explanation?"

I laugh bitterly. "Me owe *you* an explanation? You can't be serious."

"We have our problems, sure, all couples do. But we can work through it. You know how much I care about you, Cal."

How does he say that with a straight face?

"Jake, we don't need to rehash everything. It's over, we both know it. Let's just call it for what it is and move on."

Jake flies up out of the chair in frustration. "Why are you so quick to give up on this? Is this because of that guy I saw you with? The one who owns the building next door?"

I eye him suspiciously. "How do you know that?"

"You know Hopemeadow. Word gets around… what are you using him to get the space?"

I feel my jaw drop and my mouth go dry. Is that the type of woman he thinks I am? Does he really think I would do something like that?

I stand up, shaking. "This conversation is over. I'd like you to leave."

"Cal, don't. Look, I don't know what's going on, but if you're just spending time with him for now, I can be patient while you sort it out. I know you want that building. Just don't take it too far, ok?"

I'm stunned. He says it so calmly, like there is no question that I would stoop that low. Even worse, that I need his permission.

"Are you for real? Do you know how insulting that is? At least I know how to pay my own way." My hands ball into fists and my voice tightens. "Leave. *Now.*"

He stands up and fixes me in an icy stare. "You think you're so much better than everyone else, but you're not. Don't forget: this place was handed to you. You didn't earn this. The only reason you got it was because your grandma couldn't function alone anymore. So get off your high horse. You're going nowhere in this small town just like the rest of us, and some hot shot from California isn't going to be your ticket to success."

It takes all I can to muster a whisper. "Get out or I'm calling the police."

He walks out as I fall in my chair, dissolving into tears.

MY EYES still sting from crying half the afternoon, but I pull myself together. I can't let Jake get in my head. I know who I am and how hard I work. But no matter how much I know what he said isn't true, there is this small, fearful part inside of me that is afraid it could be.

For tonight, I am determined to shake it off. The first round of Christmas carols is starting soon, and I stand in line to grab our candles and song books. I haven't seen Gabe yet, and I am hoping he will still show after everything that happened the day before.

One of the local churches sponsors a warming hut after the event, and I donated a series of pies and mini tarts, along with a canteen of hot chocolate. I dropped that off quickly before coming here.

I feel a tap on the shoulder, and when I turn around, it's Jules.

"Hey! I didn't know you were coming tonight. I thought you were hanging out with Ian?"

Jules has a sparkle in her eye and smiles. "I am. He's meeting me here."

Jules and Ian have been best friends for years. They were inseparable as kids until Ian's family moved away. Every year he comes back to visit just to see her. Even now that they are adults, the tradition continues. Everyone thinks they would be a great couple and can see they are perfect for each other - except for them.

"How long is he in town for this time?"

"Only for the week. We're going to hit some of the usual events and favorites. I think he gets homesick for Hopemeadow, especially around the holidays. He's like a breath of fresh air. It's so easy to talk to him." She is beaming and brimming with excitement, talking about her plans with him, until she catches herself and stops. "I'm sorry. I forgot to ask. What happened with Jake today?" She is suddenly serious and gives me a consoling look. I hate it.

"It was fine. He's awful. We're done. I'm better now."

"Cameron said it was, and I quote, 'a disaster of epic proportions.'"

"That's one way to say it," I mutter. "But seriously, it's over, so it's fine." I give a small smile. "Really."

"I just hate that all this is happening around Christmas, you know? Couldn't he have been decent and less of a jerk until January 2nd?"

I laugh as we move forward in the line. "I'm glad he wasn't. I'd rather spend it alone than with the wrong guy. I'm in no rush for a relationship."

"Are you sure about that?" Jules says, her eyes looking mischievous.

"Yes, I'm sure."

She looks off into the crowd. "What if there was a great guy interested in you?"

I stare at her, skeptical. "Why do you say that?"

"Let's pretend. Let's say he's tall, dark, dreamy hair, chiseled jaw. He's charming, gets into it with penguins…"

"Jules…"

"And happens to be walking this way?" She nudges me and nods off in the distance. I follow her gaze and Gabe is coming towards us. He smiles and waves, and my stomach does its usual Gabe flip.

"He's leaving soon. Even if he's a great guy, there'd be no use going there." A note of sadness washes over me as I admit it.

"Well, maybe you should look at him as more of a palate cleanser then."

"Jules!" I double over laughing.

"Hear me out! He'll help you get over Jake and get you back to good so you're ready to move on. He'll be like a delicious pit stop so you're ready to move on to your next feast when you're ready." She nods her head knowingly at me like she has just come up with a brilliant plan.

"You're so ridiculous. I love you, but you're crazy." I shake my head, chuckling until I see him draw closer, staring, his eyes fixed solely on me. I whisper, "That man could never be a palate cleanser. He'd be the dessert."

Jules looks at me, surprised. "Oh dang, Callie. You *like* him."

I shake my head in denial as my heart thumps loudly, *yes*.

CHAPTER 15

GABE

"Hey, Gabe!" Jules calls out to me, waving.

"Hey! How's it going? Are you working the truck tonight?"

"Actually, no. Boss lady here gave me the night off."

"Well, isn't that generous of her," I say, looking at Callie with a grin. "Hey, Callie."

"Hi, Gabe. We're just waiting in line for the candles and song books. You got here just in time."

We reach the front of the line and get our materials, along with an extra set for a guy named Ian I haven't met yet. I am relieved to hear he isn't coming to see Callie.

We walk over near the tree that is glowing with hundreds of lights. It is stunning. Everyone is starting to light their candles, and it adds to the golden glow. Almost instantaneously, as if everyone knows what to do, voices in the crowd dim to hushed tones and murmurs.

I whisper to Callie. "It's like we stepped into a Norman Rockwell painting. Is every year like this?"

She smiles with pride. "Every year and it just keeps getting better."

A tall sandy-haired man comes up next to Jules and gives her a bear hug; this must be Ian.

The crowd starts to sing the first song, "O Christmas Tree." It is idyllic, hearing all the voices come together in unity. That is until Callie starts to sing.

"O Christmas treeee, how lovely are your branches!"

I can't believe it.

Her voice is awful.

It screeches and cracks, completely off key. I turn to look at her and she continues to sing on, loud and unabashed. I've never been a talented singer myself, but this is horrific. I am transfixed in stunned silence, watching her sing wildly out of tune, yet looking radiantly beautiful against a sea of flickering candles. She is the worst singer I have ever heard.

And in that moment, I know something has changed.

I'm falling for her.

It doesn't matter that her voice is cringeworthy. It doesn't matter that she lives across the country, or that she is cynical. None of it matters. She's smart. She makes me laugh. I feel at ease around her. She works hard and cares about her town. She isn't about appearances or trying to be someone she's not like most of the women I have dated recently. She is just Callie.

And I am all in.

She turns to look at me and smiles as she continues to sing. She must have noticed a strange look on my face.

Callie whispers, "Don't be shy. Just sing anyway. That's what I do. No one can hear you with all these people."

I suppress a laugh and wipe my hand over my mouth, trying to hide the smile that is threatening to break. Jules and I exchange a look, and she snorts. It seems Jules is aware of Callie's terrible voice, too.

"What?" Callie asks. "What's so funny?"

"Oh..." Jules says, obviously not prepared to be put on the spot. She looks around frantically and then lowers her voice.

"Mrs. Carpenter just farted," and she points to the old woman standing directly in front of us.

"Oh my goodness," Callie says as she takes two steps back.

I can't keep it in anymore and burst out laughing. Jules doubles over too, and soon the four of us are all a mess of tears and smiles.

The crowd continues to sing in serene unity, and we join in for a few more songs. When it is winding down, Jules and Ian tell us they are heading out to see a classic holiday film that is playing at the drive-in movie theatre.

"Let me know how it is!" Callie says as they are leaving. She turns to me and adds, "This is the first time they are offering short, old movies during the winter. Usually it's just a summer thing."

"Sounds like fun," I say. "Maybe we should go sometime."

Her smile fades. "That's probably not a good idea."

I start to ask her why when we are interrupted by a slight old man who looks like he is in his 70s, bundled up in a thick winter jacket, and topped off with a faded, time-worn fedora. "Callie! Dear! How have you been?"

"Lou!" She is genuinely excited to see the man and reaches over and hugs him. "How are you? How's retired life?"

"Ah, I thought I'd be saying I was bored out of my mind, but you know what? It's wonderful! No one tells you how wonderful it is." Then he leans in closer to her and whispers, "They probably just don't want to make you jealous." He winks knowingly and then looks over at me. Lou stares at me oddly, like he knows me. "Who's your new fella?"

Callie blushes and shakes her head. "He's not my... this is Gabe Montgomery. Gabe is the man who owns your old building."

"You must be related to Dominick Montgomery then?"

"Yes. That's my grandfather."

"You're the spitting image of him. It's uncanny. It's great to meet you. How is your grandfather these days? I read somewhere that he created quite the life for himself in wine country out in California."

"He did, but unfortunately he passed away a few years ago."

"I'm so sorry to hear that. He was a good man. Everyone here loved him. We were sad when he left."

"About that…" I want to see if he has any information about why my grandfather was here or what made him decide to leave when Lou starts waving frantically. I follow where he is looking and see he is gesturing to a man driving a horse and carriage.

"Ricky! Hey Ricky! I got your next customers!" He starts trotting off and pulls Callie with him.

"Lou, no, we're good. I was thinking we'd head over to the warming hut."

"Absolutely not! This young man needs to get the best view of Hopemeadow during the holidays, and that can only happen on the carriage ride."

"No, Lou, it's fine," she insists again.

"Actually, I think it looks fun," I say, my eyes twinkling at her.

She shoots me a look. "No, we're not interested. And I don't have any cash on me anyway, so we can't. Let's just get going…"

"Oh, I have cash," I offer. "I'm happy to pay." I give her a big smile and wink.

Callie sighs deeply as Lou continues to guide her closer to the carriage. "Shame on you, Callie. You know this is a Hopemeadow tradition no visitor should miss."

He nudges me. "It goes down a few streets that have the best light displays in the county. It's a real treat." Then he leans in and says, "Especially with a great little lady like Callie."

I smile at him and give him a pat on the shoulder. "I like you already, Lou."

Callie glares at me as she climbs in the carriage, making herself comfortable under the piles of wool blankets on the seats. I hop in and join her. She scoots a few inches away to make more space between us.

"It was nice to meet you, Lou! Hopefully I'll see you around again soon. I'd love to talk more about my grandfather and his time here."

"You betcha! Now have a good time, you two." He smiles and waves as the cart slowly starts to move.

"Hey Ricky," Callie says in greeting, leaning forward.

"Hi Callie! How were the carols tonight?"

"Beautiful, as always."

"That's great. It sounded good. I'll give you two a special extended tour tonight."

Callie just shakes her head and looks off into the distance, far away from me.

Once we are about a block away, the sound of the hooves hitting the pavement is almost hypnotic in its rhythmic clip clop. We turn off into a quiet neighborhood with no traffic, and it feels like we have the world all to ourselves as we view the light displays in the neighborhood.

It has been almost five minutes, and she still hasn't said anything.

"It's so peaceful here," I say, hoping to break the silence.

"It is. It's a beautiful night."

"Thank you for inviting me tonight. Everything about Hopemeadow has been a breath of fresh air... well, except for Peppermint. That penguin comes from the wrong side of the tracks."

She chuckles and I can see her shoulders relax. She shifts a bit to face forward and looks ahead. Still not quite towards me, but I'll take it.

"I'd thought about leaving Hopemeadow before. I thought that was the only way I could be happy; that I'd have to leave it all behind and start somewhere new." She stares off into the distance.

"Why did you think that?"

"As good as everyone has been to me here, there's been a lot of heartache, too. See that house up there? That's where I grew up."

Where she points stands a beautiful white colonial with black shutters and an expansive lawn. "Looks like a beautiful place to grow up."

"It was. I loved it there."

"Do your parents still live there?"

"No. My dad left when I was young and my mom died a long time ago in a car accident."

"I'm so sorry, Callie. Were you young when it happened?"

"I was 13. My grandma took me in and that's when I moved in with her in the apartment above the bakery. That's how I got started in the business. She taught me everything. When I was there and baking, I wasn't worried about anything else. It was my refuge. It felt safe…" She shakes her head. "I'm sorry, I shouldn't be sharing all of this with you."

"No, I want you to. I want to know everything about you."

She looks at me with a pained expression on her face. "Why? Why would my sad, stupid story matter to you?"

She really doesn't get it.

I take her hand in mine. She starts to pull back.

"Callie, don't."

She stops trying to pull away and looks up into my eyes, her hazel eyes glistening with tears. "Gabe, what do you want from me? I'm trying. You're making this so hard."

"How can you honestly not know? Do you not feel it?" I drop her hand and put my head in my hands in frustration.

I sit up and brace myself for whatever she might say next in response. I need to know the truth. "Am I making all this up in my head? Because if I am, please tell me."

"I'm not sure I get what you're saying."

She's still an awful liar.

I shift closer, close enough to be tormented by the sweet smell of lavender and vanilla that is pure Callie. She looks at me pleadingly and I can see there is an internal struggle that is playing out inside her.

My voice grows low and a little raspy as our eyes lock onto each other. "Forget the property. Forget your business. Forget where we live. Forget it all. Just tell me the truth. Am I in this alone? Do you feel it too?"

CHAPTER 16

CALLIE

HIS EYES SEARCH MINE FOR AN ANSWER. THE RATIONAL SIDE OF me knows I should tell him no. Giving in to temptation with Gabe can only lead to heartache. I should focus on my business and not make things more complicated. I have been fooled so many times in the past and soon Gabe will leave for California, ruining me, and any chance I have at expanding Honey's.

But as I look into his blazing blue eyes, my heart flutters, the intensity of his gaze making my entire body hum in anticipation of what I am certain will happen next.

I'm already in too deep. When I'm with him, it feels right. And I've never wanted to kiss someone as much as I do right now.

"Callie... tell me." His voice is strained and deep. "I need to hear you say it." He reaches over and cups my face in his hands, drawing me near. We are inches apart, so close I can feel the warmth of his breath dance across my lips. I can't stop myself from imagining what it would be like to close the space between us and let all of my fears go.

I touch his cheek. Shaking, daring to take the leap, I whisper, "I feel it too."

That is all he needs. He dips his head and slowly, decadently, brushes his lips across mine. He takes his time and everything about the kiss makes my pulse race. I hook my arms around his neck and arch against him, fueled by the desire for more. I rake my hands through his hair and when he breaks the kiss, it is only for a moment to stare at me in wonder before he dives back in for more. He kisses me deeper this time, with a passion that makes my toes curl, saying my name under his breath.

I love how he says my name, like it belongs on his lips, and his lips alone.

"You have no idea how badly I've wanted to do that," he says, the chemistry between us still charged in the air.

"What are we doing?" I shake my head as if to break free from a trance.

"We're enjoying a romantic horse and carriage ride," he says, smiling as he brings my hand to his lips and kisses my palm.

I smirk at him, nudging him with my shoulder. "You know what I mean. You know this is crazy, right? Nothing good can come from this."

"Good things already have," he says, as he pulls me in tight and wraps his arms around me.

THE NEXT DAY, I am still giddy. I crank up the music as I run the mixer, dumping in the ingredients for my signature jumbo blueberry muffins. I keep replaying the kiss in my mind, the sinful feeling of his mouth sealing on mine, the way his arms felt around me, holding me tight.

I felt incredible, and I never wanted it to stop.

"Ok, what's going on with you. You're beaming," Jules asks, eying me suspiciously.

I grin at her. "What do you mean? Can't a girl just be happy for no reason?"

"No," she laughs and throws her dish towel at me. "Absolutely not. What's up? What's changed? Did Gabe agree to be your silent partner?"

I bite my lip. "No."

"What else would make you so..." Jules' eyes grow wide with excitement. "OH. MY. GOODNESS! You didn't!"

I put my index finger and thumb close together. "I mean, maybe a little bit?"

"Callie!! I'm so happy for you! So are we talking a little, little, or a lotta lot?" She makes expanding and contracting signs with her hands to show small and large, wiggling her eyebrows at me.

"Jules, no!" I laugh. "It's not like that."

"I'm going to keep imagining all the things and let my mind run wild until you spill it."

"We certainly don't want that to happen," I tease.

"Sooo, what happened? Details!"

"We kissed," I say shyly.

"Ahhh!" Jules squeals. "I knew he was into you. Anyone with half a brain could see that!" She leans in eagerly. "How was it?"

"It was..." My stomach flips just thinking about it. "It was magic."

"Wow. Callie, I don't think I've seen you like this before. So, is this for real? What's going to happen now?"

"That's the part I'm trying not to think about. We made plans to meet up for lunch this afternoon. He wanted to come by for breakfast, but I had to make sure things were up and running here before playing hooky."

"Always the responsible one." She salutes me like I am her Army captain.

"Stop!" I chuckle. "You and Cameron have been working so hard keeping things going for me the past few days. I'm glad we prepared well in advance for all the events and had the deliveries lined up. I don't want things slipping here because I'm distracted."

"You don't have to worry. Everything here is good."

"I just feel like I'm setting myself up for a fall though, you know? We still haven't talked about the sale. He has valid reasons for wanting to sell and you know my reasons for wanting him not to."

"So, if one person wins, the other loses?"

"Pretty much."

"Would it really be that bad if you couldn't expand the shop? We're doing well, we're always busy."

"True, but we have so much potential. This could be even bigger and better. The only way I could expand otherwise is if I opened another shop. I can't get away like that. No one would be here with my grandma. I was lucky you could check on her while I was in Jamaica."

Jules nods, seeing the problem. "Right. She really can't be left alone for too long now. How has she been feeling lately?"

"She has her good and bad days. Being right downstairs at Honey's is ideal because I can pop up and check in on her if I know she's struggling. But I wouldn't feel good about being gone for any extended period." I look down at my hands, wringing them. "She was there for me at my darkest moment. She put her whole life on hold. I have to do the same for her. I guess I'm just trying to be greedy and have it all."

Jules comes over and hugs me. "Callie, you *can* have it all. It will work out somehow. Just enjoy things with Gabe for now. Try to be in the present. You're always so anxious that you're either dwelling on what's already happened or worried about the future. Just enjoy this for a bit. Promise me."

I smile at her. "You always know the right thing to say, you know that? You should be the next Dr. Phil."

Jules wrinkles up her nose. "No, thank you. Can I be Oprah instead?"

I laugh. "I really appreciate you always being here for me. I don't know what I'd do without you."

"Right back at ya, girl." She starts taking the croissants out of the oven. "So what is your plan for today with Gabe?"

I smile and shrug my shoulders. "I'm not sure. I have a few ideas, but I want to see if he has anything in mind."

As if on cue, the bells on the door chime. It is Gabe, looking as delicious as ever. He still has that same five o'clock shadow that drives me crazy and the minute he spots me a smile tugs at the corner of his lips.

I finish up in the kitchen and then meet him at the counter.

"May I help you, sir?" I say playfully, pretending not to know him.

"That depends. Do you happen to know a smart, beautiful woman who hates mistletoe, but loves all other things Christmas, and would be available this afternoon?"

I lean in and lower my voice seductively. "It's technically not on the menu, but yes, I think I can find someone like that for you. Come on back while I grab my coat."

We head back towards my office, but the minute we are alone he doesn't waste any time. He spins me into his arms and slides his mouth over mine, surprising me. His lips shoot sparks of heat throughout my body, and I sink into it, running my hands down his strong back, delighting in the feel of him. He pulls away and gives me a lopsided grin.

"Had to make sure I gave you a proper hello."

"You'll get no complaints from me." I nibble at his lips playfully and then go behind my desk to get my coat.

Gabe picks up a picture frame from my desk.

My heart swells every time I look at that picture. "That's my grandma, Alice. She's the one who started all this."

He looks between me and the photo. "She was beautiful. You look a lot like her."

"Thank you. She was a force to be reckoned with."

"Oh, I'm sorry. When did she pass away?"

"Oh, goodness, I didn't mean to imply that she died. She has just changed so much over the past couple years. It started with a few nasty falls that had her laid up for a while, and then I noticed she was growing increasingly more forgetful. That's when we learned she has the beginning stages of Alzheimers. Friends come to visit her, but she hasn't been leaving the apartment as much as she used to. Some days are better than others, but recently I've seen more of a decline."

"I'm so sorry. That must be very hard to watch someone you love go through that."

I nod. "On her bad days… it breaks my heart. She's a shadow of the woman she used to be." I pause and then reluctantly add, "I actually live with her upstairs above the bakery. I used to have my own place and would run up and check in on her throughout the day, but when she kept falling, I decided it would be best for me to move back in so I could keep a closer eye on her and she wouldn't be alone."

"She's lucky to have you. Do you have anyone else who helps?"

"Not yet. My sister Willa was supposed to come into town for Christmas so we could discuss it, but it sounds like she is trying to back out now."

"How many siblings do you have?"

"Just the one sister and she's in New York. She's five years older than me, so when my mom died, she decided to go away to college. She has stayed away ever since. I think it's hard for her to visit Hopemeadow since she died, but now I can't handle the bakery and caring for my grandma all on my own. I'd love for her to move back, but it probably won't happen."

Gabe nods. "I can see how all of that would be overwhelming." He reaches out and grabs my hand, giving it a gentle squeeze.

I shake my head and smile. "It's all ok and actually, I was

going to tell you that we need to keep this afternoon short. I haven't had time to spend with her lately. I haven't even decorated the apartment for Christmas yet, so I thought I could get a little tree and spruce things up at the apartment a bit and hopefully boost her spirits."

"That sounds fun. I'm in."

I chuckle. "I wasn't asking you to do it with me. I just wanted you to know that I'll have to leave early and head back."

"I know. I was inviting myself. Since someone convinced me to hang out here in Hopemeadow, I haven't had a chance to put up a tree. It doesn't feel like Christmas without a tree, Callie." His blue eyes glint, teasing me.

I start to agree and then reconsider. "That's probably not a good idea."

"I feel like you've said that to me a lot since we've met." He walks over to the door and shuts it behind him, closing us in.

"We haven't even had a real first date yet. Are we skipping a few steps here?"

"I have an idea: let's stop worrying about all the reasons we shouldn't do things and just do whatever we want."

He smiles at me wickedly and walks over with a mischievous look in his eye. My heart races. He puts his hand under my chin and tilts my face up to his.

"What is it exactly that you want?" I say in a half whisper.

He brushes his hands down my arms and takes both of my hands in his, pressing the length of his body to mine. My skin tingles with his touch.

"Just one thing," he murmurs. "You."

He dives in to kiss me with a need that sends me reeling. I kiss him back, giving in, and for the moment, letting go.

GABE

"Try not to swoon as you watch me be super masculine and saw down this tree," I say, trying to deflect from the fact that I have no idea what I am doing and have never used a saw before.

"Manual labor is sexy. Especially when I'm not the one doing it," she jokes.

I wink at her as I take the saw to the base of the tree and begin to cut.

The tree farm Callie took us to is on the other side of the mountain, past the Hillside Inn where I am staying. I naively assumed we would go to a church parking lot somewhere and select a pre-cut tree. Apparently, that's not what you do in Hopemeadow. Here, you go all Paul Bunyan and cut it down yourself.

I will admit, this farm is epic. But there are over 60 acres of Christmas trees to choose from, and it takes Callie an hour to pick one out. An entire hour. This one is too big; that one is too small. Some look tilted, others she said would die within the week. They all look basically the same to me, but Callie has a vision of what she wants and won't settle until she finds it. I'm not sure if I will ever feel my toes again, but it is worth it to see the smile on her face as she stares at her perfect tree.

"You're doing great! It's starting to tip!" she yells excitedly.

I get it to the point where it is almost completely cut through. I stand up, push it the rest of the way over, and we watch it crash to the ground.

Callie cheers, leaps over, and hugs me. Basking in the glow of her happiness, I feel invigorated just being with her. I kiss her and she nuzzles my nose.

"That was my first time cutting down a tree. You're giving me new life experiences here."

"Please don't tell me you're one of those guys who has an artificial tree!"

"Well…" I hedge.

"Ahhh… la la la la, I'm not listening!" Callie plugs her ears and pretends she can't hear me. "I don't want to know."

Still laughing and dodging the question, I drag the tree over to the side of the path so we can wait for the tractor to come back around and grab us.

I wrap my arms around her to keep us warm. "You really love Christmas, don't you?"

I can see the tractor coming in the distance, which is good because my fingers are almost frozen solid.

"Yes, and I especially love all the traditions. In a world where nothing is certain, there's something comforting knowing that some things stay the same. It brings together all of my favorite things: family, friends, and good food. Not to mention it's a fantastic time for Honey's."

Callie's face drops at the thought of the bakery. She looks uncomfortable and then turns to look at me. "Can I ask you something?"

"Anything."

She bites her lip. "Have you looked at the proposal I gave you?"

"Yes, I have."

"And? What do you think?"

I sigh. "Callie, let's not talk about business right now, ok?"

"It's just… you haven't started the process of selling the building yet, right?"

I hesitate, not wanting to ruin the moment, but also know I need to be honest. "No, I haven't, but there have been three interested parties who have looked at it and offers are likely."

"Ok." She plays with her hair nervously. "So, when should we talk about it?"

"I'm here for another four days."

"Four days??" she says, incredulous. "That's it?"

"I've already stayed longer than I planned. I have been pushing off meetings and I have to take care of a few things. But I'm planning on coming back. We'll figure something out, ok?"

She doesn't respond. She looks distressed, as if she is trying to push whatever she is feeling down deep and not show it.

I take her face in my hands and guide it to mine. "Can we make the next few days about us and nothing else? Please? I won't pull the rug out from under you. I will tell you before I move forward with anything regarding the property. I just want to enjoy this time with you without anything else clouding it."

She looks at me reluctantly as the tractor pulls up to bring us back to the store to pay and tie up the tree. "I'll try. But keep in mind, that's going to take a lot of distractions. You better bring your A game."

"You're in luck. Distractions are my specialty." I lean in and wrap my arms around her, hugging her tight.

I don't want to think about the future either.

"WE ALMOST GOT IT! Just lift it a little higher over the railing and it shouldn't get stuck this time," Callie says from the top of the stairs. Getting this giant tree into her apartment is a fiasco. Had I been to her place before, I would have known how narrow the stairwell is and would have suggested something much smaller, not a tree that rivals the one in Rockefeller Center.

"How in the world did you think this monster tree would fit in this little stairwell?" I growl from below as I lift it higher.

"I've been doing this for years! Where there's a will, there's a way! Worst case, we can rig some sort of pulley system and get it in through a window."

I give her a death stare, and she cracks up laughing.

"We're fine! It's almost there! One more good lift and push! Ahhh, we got it!" The tree plops down and falls onto her kitchen floor. I turn to look back down the stairs and there's a sea of needles behind us. I don't know how any still remain on the tree.

Callie is grinning ear to ear, thrilled. Her genuine excitement makes it easy to let go of my crankiness about the tree. She is radiant. I'd do anything to see that smile.

"Wait here, let me go check on my grandma. She didn't come out yet, so she may be resting."

She disappears down a hallway, and I take a seat at the kitchen table. There is no doubt someone's grandmother lives here. Everything about the kitchen has a retro aesthetic and makes you feel like you have been thrown back in time. The appliances are an avocado green and match the patterned wallpaper on the walls. The delicious aroma from the bakery drifts up from below. I imagine it must be the best kind of torture to smell that all day.

Callie returns and says, "She's laying down now, so why don't we get the tree up in the stand and I'll pull out all the ornaments."

A half hour later, the tree is up in the corner of the living room and the floor is littered with boxes of ornaments. Callie wants to wait a bit to see if her grandmother feels up to decorating with us when she wakes. We sit on the couch together, taking a break, and drinking a cup of coffee.

"So, you said your grandma was the original owner of Honey's? Did she encourage you to take it over?"

"After my mom died, I think my grandma used teaching me about baking as a way to keep me busy. If I wasn't in school, I was at the bakery, learning or working. It was never forced, and I loved it. She was self-taught and had come so far. When I was 18, my first car wasn't actually a car. It was the food truck."

I laugh, surprised. "Seriously?"

"Yes! She inspired me. We didn't have a lot of money and I needed to pay for college, so I started Honey's Treat Truck. At that point, I had no plans to take over the bakery and was working towards a degree in business. Every morning, I'd load up the truck and drive it to Hartford and sit outside State House Square during the morning rush. Then I'd head off to classes."

"An entrepreneur from the start."

"It paid my way through college and then by the time I graduated, all I could think about were ways to improve Honey's. I tried a few different jobs, but I didn't want the traditional 9 to 5 at a desk. I was miserable. When my grandma started falling more, she was about to close up the shop until I said I would step in. I knew she was secretly thrilled about it, but she never wanted me to feel pressure about continuing the family business."

I pick up one of the old photo albums on the coffee table and flip through it. "Let's get a closer look at Callie as a little girl, shall we?"

"Ahh no, no, no. Enough of that," Callie says, laughing as she tries to take the album from my hands.

I lean back and keep it at a distance. "Not so fast! There must be something good in here if you don't want me to see it."

She lunges at me again, falling on top of me, desperately trying to get to it.

"You're never going to get it, but man, I like how you're trying. You can stay here as long as you want." I wink at her and extend my arm out further so that the album is just out of reach.

"Gah, fine!" She sits up and playfully swats at me. "Just know that I went through a rough phase from the ages of 8 to 13. I hold no responsibility as I was not the one making decisions about my hair or choice of clothing."

I laugh and flip through the first few pages. "Is that you with your grandma at the bakery?"

"Yes, that was right after I moved in here," she says.

"Wow, you've done a lot with the place. It has changed a lot."

"I've tried to modernize it over the years. I want to make it my own. I can really relate to what you were saying about your grandfather and needing to make your own way. I didn't want to feel like I didn't earn it, you know?"

"Yes. I know exactly what you mean."

Just as I am flipping through to another page, the door to the bedroom opens. Callie's grandmother stands in the doorway, looking tired and frail. She has a knit shawl wrapped around her shoulders that she holds pinched together with one hand and, in the other, she clutches a cane to help steady her. I can see she has the same beautiful hazel eyes as Callie, but hers look worn and sad, until she sees me. Her eyes light up and a joyous smile brightens her face.

"Dominick?" She looks at me as if she were looking at a ghost. She reaches out her hand gently towards me. "Is that you?"

"No Grandma, this is Gabe Montgomery. Gabe, this is my grandmother, Alice Parker."

She called me Dominick.

"Nice to meet you, Mrs. Parker."

"You look just like him. It's… you look just like him."

"Grandma, maybe you should go back in and lay down."

Callie stands to help escort her grandmother back to bed when I stop her.

"Dominick is my grandfather. Did you know him?"

"Yes, he was a wonderful man. He was very special to me." She reaches towards the nearby armchair and Callie carefully guides her down. Although she is still faintly smiling, tears well in her eyes as she stares off into the distance.

"How did you two know each other? His time here in Hope-meadow, and how he came to own the building next door, was always a bit of a mystery to my family. He never seemed to want to talk about it. That's part of the reason I'm here; I'd love to know more about that time in his life."

Alice shakes her head. She is choked up with emotion.

"It's ok if you're not feeling up to talking, Mrs. Parker. I'm sorry if we woke you. We picked up a tree and thought we'd get things out for you if you were up for decorating tonight."

Alice shakes her head again and pulls a tissue out of her pocket, dabbing at her eyes. She reaches over to the coffee table and picks up one of the smaller photo albums. Flipping it over to access the pocket in the back cover, she pulls out a worn black-and-white photo and hands it to Callie. "He was my first love."

Callie freezes, her eyes going wide as she looks at the photo and then at me.

It is a photo of Alice and my grandfather, Dominick, laughing and hugging at a park.

"I had no idea you loved anyone other than Grandpa." Callie looks shocked at the revelation.

"Dominick was in Connecticut for a summer internship while he was in college. We met and.... it was magic. It was as if we had known each other for years. We were inseparable. By the end of the summer, we wanted to get married. He used his inheritance and bought the building next door for us. He furnished it and was making plans to stay when he asked my father for his blessing."

"What happened?"

Alice sighs and shakes her head slowly. "My father said no. He thought he wouldn't be able to take care of me. He didn't like Dominick's career plans and thought he was too much of a risk taker. He said he was careless and that he didn't take our future seriously. I begged my father, but he said he would never allow it."

"Oh Grandma, I never knew."

"We were crushed, but Dominick didn't want to drive a wedge between me and my family. He wanted to do the right thing, so he left and went with one of his friends out to California. We wrote letters for a while, but it became too painful to continue talking to him. I was devastated that he left and convinced myself that meant he didn't really love me. A few years later I met your grandfather, and we started a family. Yes, I loved your grandfather, but Dominick? He was my soulmate."

"That's why he never sold the building. He couldn't let it go." It is all finally starting to make sense.

"I didn't realize he was still the owner. I thought he sold it when he left. He had it up for sale for a while, but must have never gone through with it."

Callie reaches out and grabs my hand. I look at her and it hits me, that all these years later, I am in Hopemeadow falling for her, thanks to my grandfather.

Alice sees us holding hands and looks surprised, but doesn't comment on it.

"Dominick tried to get in contact with me years later after my father died, but by then I was married. I think he was hoping we could reconnect and was hurt that I had moved on. I didn't think he was coming back, and I had made a commitment to Phillip. It was too late."

"I can't believe I'm just finding out about this now. Why haven't you talked about this before?"

"I didn't want to confuse you, dear, but I'm glad you know now." Alice drops her head and takes a deep breath, mustering up the courage and energy she needs. "Losing Dominic is my biggest regret in life. I let circumstances and other people get in the way. I should have fought for him. I just didn't realize."

"Didn't realize what, Grandma?"

"That none of the rest of it matters without love."

I look over at Callie as she hugs her grandmother tight.

None of the rest of it matters.

CHAPTER 18

GABE

WE SPEND THE NEXT HOUR DECORATING THE TREE. CALLIE IS A pro with the lights. Every ornament has a story, and the tree contains a lifetime of memories. Alice helped with the ornaments for a while and then retreated to her room to rest. I caught her staring at us periodically, and it made me wonder if she was envisioning the past.

When we finish, Callie and I return to the couch, turn on some Christmas music, dim the lights, and stare at the tree together. She leans over and rests her head on my shoulder, our bodies side by side, curled into each other.

"I can't believe our grandparents were in love. Isn't that crazy? What are the odds? If I didn't see the photo myself, I wouldn't have believed it."

"Selfishly, I'm very glad it didn't work out."

"Ditto." Callie laughs and then grows serious. "She spent her whole life with another man and not with her true love. She always seemed happy with my grandfather, but I guess you never know what people are hiding deep inside."

"None of us knew about my Gramps and Alice, either. He

never talked about it, but after all those years he still couldn't let go of the building." I groan. "And yet here I am about to sell it."

My mind races as I think about why he would have left it to me. Did he want me to know about Alice? What was he trying to tell me?

Callie grows quiet and says, "The money from that sale could really help you. You have a dream. You should go after it."

I sit up and look at her, stunned. "You don't mean that."

"I do. I already have my dream. I wake up and I do what I love every day. Yes, I want more and I see so many ways I can improve, but I don't *need* it. In this moment, I'm happy. I want that for you, too."

I stare into her eyes and feel my heart explode into a million pieces. This woman is selflessly giving me permission to move forward with the sale, forgoing her dream for mine.

"Callie, are you sure about this? I know I said we should wait to talk about it, but I've been thinking about your proposal and..."

"Don't." She puts her hands up in a stop motion. "I'm sure. You should invest in that vineyard. Go with your gut and chase your dream. I could never forgive myself if I selfishly took that from you just to make mine bigger. Just keep your promise that you won't sell to Bon Bon's, ok?" She gives me a genuine smile, takes my hand, and slings it over her shoulder. "Now that that's settled, back to this tree. I see a couple spots where there is crowding and then others that are empty. I think we're going to have to do some rearranging..."

I laugh, shaking my head.

This woman is everything I could ever want and more. Why would I walk away? I don't want to make the same mistake my grandfather did. I know if I invest the money into that vineyard, I can prove myself worthy again to my family. But what would that do for me if I didn't have Callie? I stare at her, bathed in the glow of the colored lights, while she analyzes the tree, talking about how she plans to improve it with little tweaks. Ever the perfectionist, always planning. Always making things better for everyone around her.

She's the one.

I can't go back to the way things were.

I have never been more certain of anything in my entire life. It is both terrifying and exhilarating.

I lean over and kiss her forehead, gently playing with a strand of her hair. I make a mental note to phone Abby to call off the sale and to start looking for a contractor.

I have a new plan that needs to be put into motion.

CHAPTER 19

GABE

"What's it going to take for you to finally come join me on the east coast?"

I shake my head at Will and laugh. This is becoming an old joke with my brother. Whenever we get together, we try to convince the other one to move. It is like a reflex.

But now, I am actually planning on it.

We are on our second beer at a bar in Blue Back Square in West Hartford. He lives in upstate New York and I rarely get a chance to see him, so we both made the trip tonight to catch up in person. No matter the distance, he is my best friend, and it feels great to be in the same room again.

Will leans back in his chair and smirks. "It's only a matter of time before Mom drives you nuts and you flee like I did."

"Eh, it's not that bad. She just gets worried about us and channels it into overzealous meddling. I've found it's manage-able in small doses. Plus, you must have forgotten about all the wine she's constantly dropping off. It helps ease the crazy."

Will laughs. "True." He lifts his beer for a toast. "To easing the crazy!" We clink our glasses together and take a sip.

I'm not sure how he will react to my latest news, so I

contemplate my next words carefully. "Maybe it's time I come out here and see what New England has to offer."

Will sits up straight and looks confused. "Wait, what? Seriously?"

"Seriously. This week has been an eye-opener. Maybe it's time for something new. I could envision myself out here."

Will frowns. "What gives? Why the sudden change?"

"Thanks for the warm welcome, bro," I say, sarcasm dripping from my voice. "I thought you'd be happy."

"It's not that. You know I'd love to have you out here. I could destroy you in basketball every weekend and remind you who's the boss. But something's different." One eyebrow shoots up as he crosses his arms. "Is it that girl who runs the bakery? The one who's trying to convince you to go into business with her?"

"Her name's Callie."

"So, that's a yes. You meet this girl and within a week you're willing to move here? She must be pretty talented." He lays on the sarcasm thick.

"It's not like that. She's different from all the other women I've met."

Will looks at me, skeptical, not saying anything.

Frustrated, I sigh. "Look, I know what you're thinking. You should come by Honey's and meet her. You can see for yourself."

This gets his attention. "The bakery she owns is Honey's? I think I've heard of that place. It's supposed to be fantastic. Does she have a food truck that goes to events in Hartford sometimes?"

"Yeah, that's the place. But here's the crazy part. You know how I told you Gramps was in love with a woman named Alice while he was here?"

Will nods. "I still can't believe that. You have to tell me what Mom says when you tell her. Better yet, I want to be on video when you do it, so I can see her face. I'll make popcorn first."

I laugh, kicking him under the table. "Focus, man! There's more."

"Do we have some crazy long-lost relative out there? If so, I'm going to need another beer." He scans the room for our waitress.

"No! Are you ready for this? Alice is Callie's grandmother."

Will's mouth drops open. "What?"

"Yeah, Callie had no idea about it either until last night. Alice showed us a photo of them together."

"That's crazy." He pauses. "Or is it a little convenient?"

"How is that convenient?"

"Let's back up a minute. What does all of this have to do with you suddenly wanting to move out here? A few weeks ago, all you could talk about was your plan for that new vineyard. You're still moving forward with it, right?"

I take a deep breath. "No."

"No?? Why not?"

"I'm going to become her partner at Honey's. She gave me her business proposal. It looks great and when I ran the numbers, it's a smart move. Probably not the windfall investing in the vineyard would be, but with time it could really be something special."

"Woah, do you hear yourself right now?" He points at me. "You want to know what I think?"

Here we go.

"Nope."

He leans in on the edge of his seat. "That's alright, I'm telling you anyway."

I groan. "Surprise, surprise. Here comes the lecture."

"It's not a lecture. It's my job to be the heavy. It sounds like she's using you."

"No, she's not. You don't know her. She even told me last night that I should sell the building. She cares about me. I'm telling you, she's different. She's beautiful, intelligent, and caring. She's a… force."

Will looks unconvinced. "A force? That's an interesting way to describe someone."

"Don't get me wrong, she can be a little intense and is definitely a workaholic. Kind of cynical and a bit too cautious…"

"Gee, she sounds like a lot of fun. I'd move across the country for that." He rolls his eyes.

I laugh. "No, I just… I can't describe it. It feels like I've known her my whole life."

"You've got it bad for this girl." Will pauses to think. "But how would you even fit in to her world? You can't even make scrambled eggs. You'd be useless in a bakery."

"I was thinking I could take my knowledge of the wine business and we could turn Honey's into a dual bakery wine bar. It would add a nighttime element that could bring in a lot of new business. The shop is right off of the Connecticut wine trail too, so it could potentially bring in a lot of business from out of town."

Skeptical, Will says, "And she's open to changing her entire business model?"

"Well…" I hedge. "I haven't presented it to her yet. But I will. I'm sure she'll love it. I was going to look into the renovation costs and meet with a few contractors to get a better idea of the project first."

"Don't you think that's putting the cart before the horse? Have you thought this through?"

"It will work out. I know it will."

Will rakes his hand through his shaggy brown hair, clearly not on board with my plan. "No, hear me out. You never look at the big picture. How is all this going to work?"

"We'll figure it out."

"You drive me crazy with this idealistic, impulsive garbage. Don't go planning your entire life around this without making sure she's in it too, and for the right reasons. You say you want to be with her, but you just met her. You need to slow down, man. Get to know her. You never think and then you're shocked when things don't work out."

"Hey, easy killer. I think. I'm just a man of action and don't stall when I want something. I go with my gut."

"Your gut isn't always right. Remember Sadie?"

I sigh. "Callie's nothing like Sadie."

"You trust too quickly. You almost married her. She would have taken you for a ride if things had been different."

"Well, the minute she learned I wasn't getting the vineyard, that settled that, didn't it?" I say bitterly.

"I think Gramps knew. He knew leaving the estate to Mom would make Sadie leave. Sadie was as opportunistic as they come. He did you a favor changing his will like that."

"No," I say quietly. "That's not why he did it. It had nothing to do with my relationship with Sadie. I made mistakes. I didn't prove myself and he didn't trust me anymore."

Will shakes his head vigorously. "Gabe, you were young. Gramps didn't hold that against you. He was trying to protect you. After everything you've found out this week, why can't you see that now? He left you that building because he wanted you to come here and learn about his past. He didn't want you to end up with a selfish woman like Sadie or have any regrets in the future."

"Why are you bringing all this up now? That's history. I haven't talked to Sadie in years."

"This Callie girl, she sounds great and all, but don't let her be another Sadie. Did you ever consider she might be after you just for the building? You trust too quickly. Don't give up everything for someone you just met."

I cup my hand to my mouth and call out to no one in partic- ular in the bar. "Can someone get this Grinch another drink? He's bringing me down over here."

I hear a smattering of laughter. Will continues on anyway, serious. "Just keep an eye out for red flags. Maybe she's great. I haven't met her, but I know you. And I know you tend to jump in with both feet before thinking it through. You can be too loyal and that kind of generosity can be manipulated if someone wants to capitalize on it."

"Man, all these compliments sandwiched between a ton of insults. My self-esteem is skyrocketing."

"I love you, man. Just protect yourself."

"Ok, enough of the big brother protective nonsense. I hear you. I'll be careful. Stop pouring out your heart and scolding me. It's not a good look." I take another sip of my drink and change the subject. "What about you? Aren't you supposed to be the idealistic one? Aren't all teachers supposed to inspire people with their uplifting mumbo jumbo?"

"If you saw what I dealt with every day, you wouldn't be hopeful for the future."

"Yikes. That's bleak. How's Alina?"

"I don't want to talk about it." He tosses the rest of his drink back in one swig.

"Wait, are you kidding? You just spent however long schooling me about my relationship and now you don't want to talk about yours? No way. Your turn."

He looks down at his empty glass, his head hanging low. "We're getting a divorce."

"What? I'm so sorry. What happened?"

"We haven't been happy for a while… and it spiraled out of control."

"You guys were so good before."

"Yeah, I know. Things aren't always what they seem."

I take a sip of my beer as he launches into the story of the demise of his marriage, and I try to push any doubts about Callie's intentions far from my mind.

CHAPTER 20

CALLIE

IT HAS BEEN SNOWING HARD MOST OF THE AFTERNOON. I SPENT the morning taking care of things at the bakery, but I promised Doris I would pop over to the inn and drop off a tray of cookies for her, along with a few loaves of bread, so she would be stocked for the weekend. She routinely orders baked goods from me for her guests at Hillside, and I am grateful for her continued loyalty. Since we are under a storm watch, I don't want her to attempt to drive to the shop to pick it up. I've seen her drive and let's just say it's scary, even without bad weather.

It looks like the roads are quickly deteriorating, so I lock up the bakery and send Jules and Cameron home early. My plan is to drop these off and head home for the night and get snowed in with my grandma. She has been doing so well since Gabe visited, and I think it makes her happy that we are together. She even has a few friends over this evening for a small holiday party. It is almost as if being reminded of her former love with Dominick and our hope at happiness reinvigorates her. She seems to have more energy, and I heard her singing Christmas carols as she got dressed. With Alzheimers, days like this are a blessing. She is so much more like herself. It is wonderful, and I feel I owe it all to Gabe.

My little Prius trudges up the hill towards the inn reluctantly, wheels spinning and sliding, then finally catching along the way. Even though I can see tracks where the road has been plowed earlier, the snow is coming down so fast I am having trouble gaining traction.

I am starting to get nervous that I won't make it up the hill when I finally reach the top and pull into the parking lot.

I bring in Doris's order and place it on the front desk. "Hi Doris! Just dropping this off quick! I threw in a pumpkin pie for you for some extra holiday cheer."

"Oh you sweet girl, thank you!" Doris calls out as she comes out from the back. "I can't believe you braved this storm for me! I'm glad you made it through because I just heard on the police scanner the bottom of the mountain is at a stand still. Sounds like there was a nasty accident."

"Oh no! Do you think I'll be able to get through?"

"I'm not sure. I don't think you should risk it in that tiny car of yours."

"But the storm is supposed to worsen through the night. I can't get trapped up here. I was hoping to get snowed in with my grandma. We're going to watch 'It's a Wonderful Life' together. It's her favorite."

"Could you call one of the girls and see if they can check in on her? I really don't think it's safe for you to be going down the mountain in this. I'd never forgive myself if something happened to you!"

"I could see if Jules could walk over. She lives right on Main, so it probably wouldn't be too bad for her. Would it be ok if I hung out here in the lobby until the worst of it is over?"

"Why, that's silly, Callie! You are standing in one of Connecticut's finest inns. Lucky for you, I have an available cabin you can stay in, on me."

"Oh, I couldn't possibly!"

"Of course you can! I can even send you up there with soup and some of that delicious bread you brought me."

"You are so kind, Doris. Thank you so much. I really appreciate it. I'll head out first thing in the morning assuming the roads are clear."

"No rush! It's my pleasure." She digs around behind the desk for a moment. "Ah, yes. Cabin four. Actually, you'll be right next door to your friend, Mr. Montgomery. Maybe the two of you can play a few board games… or something." Her eyes twinkle as she hands me the key, smiling.

Butterflies take flight in my stomach. It hadn't dawned on me that I could be getting snowed in with Gabe. He texted me last night before he met up with his brother and said he wanted to see me soon, but we hadn't made an official plan. I'm not sure if he is even here, but the thought of seeing him makes me feel giddy.

Giddy and nervous, my mind begins racing with what-if's and possibilities. I try to push it all out of my head and thank Doris again profusely as she hands me a bag with the soup, sample sized toiletries, and a few towels.

I trudge out into the middle of the winter wonderland that is in full effect all around me. The skies have opened up. The snow is coming down hard, the wind whipping and howling, making it difficult to see too far ahead. I hurry and make my way over to cabin four. Right beside me at cabin five, I see Gabe's rental car.

Rental car. Right. Because he doesn't live here, is going to leave, and I'll never see him again.

My heart sinks. I can't allow myself to think about it. If I fall down that rabbit hole, I may never come out.

I make my way inside. It has been a long time since I stepped foot in one of these cabins, and I am impressed again by the cozy, rustic vibe. I feel a tinge of excitement at the thought of having a night to myself here. Staying with my grandma is nice, but a whole night alone in my own place? That sounds amazing.

I pull my coat tight and shiver. Even though I am inside, it isn't much warmer in here. I can't find a thermostat, so I attempt to start a fire. It is a modern propane fireplace, but I can't get it to light. It seems simple enough to operate, but after multiple attempts, I wonder if it is out of propane. I run back over to the main lodge and find that Doris has already locked up for the night.

The snow is blinding. I don't want to make Doris feel like she has to come out here and help me figure this out. She has already been so generous letting me stay here. Freezing, I know I only have one option left.

I trudge through the snow over to Gabe's cabin, take a deep, calming breath, and knock.

The door swings open and there is Gabe, shirtless in a towel, his dark hair still wet from the shower. It is all I can do to keep my eyes up and not let them drift.

For goodness sakes, control yourself, Callie.

In the presence of this beautiful man, I stumble for words. "Um, hi. I'm so sorry, I probably should have called first."

"No, it's fine." He grins at me. "It's freezing though, and I'm in an open doorway in what feels like the frozen tundra. Come in?"

He moves aside just enough for me to get through, and as I enter, the back of my hand grazes his stomach. Being near him is unnerving on a regular day, so seeing him shirtless and glistening right now feels like sensory overdrive.

I pretend to fidget with my coat and divert my eyes down to sneak a peek at the rippled muscles in his stomach.

Oh, man. Suddenly, I'm not freezing anymore.

Stay calm. This is no big deal. Just keep it together.

"I'm sorry for barging in on you like this. I dropped off an order to Doris and now the bottom of the mountain is a mess from the storm. Doris said I could crash here for the night."

Gabe's eyebrows jump up, and he throws me a wicked smile. "There's only one bed in here, but that's ok with me if it's ok with you."

I stammer, "No, not here, here, I mean the inn itself. She gave me the key to cabin four next door... I wasn't inviting myself to stay in your cabin."

He laughs heartily. "I love messing with you. You make it so easy."

I smirk and throw my scarf at him. "Ha, ha, funny guy. I couldn't get my fireplace to start and I was an icicle over there."

He walks over and steps behind me, easing me out of my coat. As he is helping me take it off, he leans over and murmurs low in my ear. "I couldn't have asked for a better surprise than seeing you at my door."

A shiver courses through me as I feel the warmth of his breath down my neck. I try to compose myself.

"Anyhow, I know I'm interrupting. I was hoping you could help me get it started? I'm not sure if it's user error or if it's out of propane."

He takes my coat and tosses it on the dresser beside his bed. "Sure I can." He rubs his hand on his chest absentmindedly, thinking.

Goodness, man. Please get dressed. I can't take this torture.

"Although," he continues, looking inspired, "why don't you just hang out here with me? It's already nice and warm in here."

I smile at him, suddenly feeling shy. "I'm not sure that's a good idea."

He tilts his head to the side, confused, and then looks down at himself. "Am I making you uncomfortable because I'm in a towel?"

I sputter out quickly, in one shot, "Oh, of course not. I'm fine. Fine. Really, it's fine. You're totally covered. Nothing more than I'd see on a beach somewhere. Or a pool. Heck, if you were going running, it would be the same thing, right? Probably wouldn't want to run in a towel, though. Those things aren't very sturdy." I flash a nervous smile to be extra convincing.

He snickers. "Yes, you're so very fine. Why don't I get dressed and then we can figure out what to do about your fireplace?"

He disappears into the bathroom and I collapse down onto his bed in a huff, shaking my head in embarrassment.

Why am I so awkward?!

The door to the bathroom starts to open and I bolt upright, quickly posing myself in a casual lean to the side, so I look calm and at ease.

He comes out still in his towel, chuckling, "Kind of hard to get dressed without my clothes."

I barely hear what he says. My breath catches at the sight of him.

He is everything a man should be.

It's not just physical. Yes, this man is gorgeous. But he is also considerate, funny, charming, and kind. He seems to anticipate my needs and how I'm feeling before I'm even aware of it. And here he is, standing before me, reminding me just how incredible he really is, inside and out.

But I'm not a saint. I bite my lip, remembering what it is like to kiss him. How he is both gentle and commanding all at once. How he is passionate and giving, but very much in control. He's not in a hurry, or trying to push things to a different level.

He's just right there in the moment, making me feel adored.

I feel wanted for who I am and it makes all the difference.

My thoughts must be written all over my face as our eyes lock. He grows suddenly serious, and the intensity in his stare sends a jolt of electricity through me.

I have to get out of here or I won't be able to fight this

anymore. I get up and start walking towards the door. "I'll just meet you over there once you're ready, ok?"

He doesn't answer and instead follows me.

"Callie." I love how he says my name. His voice is gruff. Urgent. Almost like he is in pain.

I turn, reluctant. "Gabe, I..."

I don't have time to finish. He grabs me, guiding me back against the doorframe, devouring me, wrapping his arms around my waist. His hunger for me feels raw. I shudder, craving him in return.

He picks me up, and I wrap myself around him as we kiss. I am frantic to feel more, to be closer to him.

He bites at my lip and the kiss deepens, both of us breathless and surprised by the tidal wave of emotion that consumes us. He takes his time, nibbling at my neck, trailing up to my ear, and then working his way over to my mouth, kissing me with such passion I feel dizzy.

He carries me across the room to a chair, placing me on the edge, and kneels down in front of me. He grasps both of my wrists in his hands, stopping me from reaching for him further.

He traces me with his eyes, not touching me, just taking me in.

There is no more pretending. How I feel about him radiates from my soul. It's a raw vulnerability that is exciting and terrifying all at once.

The intimacy of his gaze, of staring into each other's eyes without pretense, is almost unnerving.

My voice is barely a whisper when I say, "Why are you looking at me like that?"

"I'm the luckiest man alive. I want to remember every moment of this," he says, his voice almost a growl. "I'm going to take my time and enjoy every moment I get with you. Is that ok?"

I merely nod in reply. He continues to look at me, lightly

trailing his fingers down my cheek, cupping my face, running his fingers through my hair. He's inches from me and I can smell his cologne and feel the warmth of his breath on my skin. His mouth curves into a slow smile, and mine mirrors his in response.

It is then that I know. I'll never be able to come back from this, from him, from all that is building between us.

My life is forever changed.

Gabe's eyes come back to mine as he caresses my cheek, placing another soft kiss on my lips. He murmurs, "I'm never letting you go."

I'm speechless. My heart is racing and it feels like it will beat out of my chest. I reach out for him, kissing him again. I don't want to think any more. I don't want to question what I am doing or why. I just want to be with him in this moment.

Together, tonight, the powerful connection between us surpasses the raging storm outside.

CHAPTER 21

CALLIE

My eyes blink open and the first thing I see is Gabe asleep beside me, mouth slightly parted, his gorgeous face at ease.

I study him and feel my body fill with a warmth and contentment I have never known. We spent the night wrapped in each other's arms, talking, laughing, and sharing. And now, waking up with him feels like I have started a new life, one filled with hope and possibility.

For once, I'm not scared. Everything inside me proclaims he's the one, and I finally let my guard down. Gabe is attentive, kind, smart, and funny. He's supportive and loving. He's not afraid to say how he feels. He's the man dreams are made of; why would I ever fight that? I have been denying this feeling for so long, and now I'm kicking myself for not giving in sooner. Even with all the hurdles we might face, this doesn't feel risky.

It feels right.

I reach over and snuggle into him, resting my head on his chest. He instinctively curls towards me, wrapping me in his arms, and sighs. His eyes blink open and he looks down at me with a sleepy grin.

"Hey you." He rubs his eyes. "Are you watching me while I sleep?"

"If I say yes, does that make me a creeper?"

"Yes."

"Then no, I definitely wasn't."

I snuggle in deeper, grinning like a fool, and put my arm around his waist. I lay on him, feeling content, enjoying the warmth of this perfect moment, when my stomach growls loudly with an extended rumble and churning.

Gabe chuckles. "Guess someone has an appetite."

I poke him playfully and say, "I skipped dinner last night and went straight for dessert."

"Am I this dessert you're speaking of? Are you objectifying me, Callie?"

"Yes, yes, I am. You're a delicious man treat."

He roars with laughter. "I hope I'm a little more than that."

"Yes, you're much more than that. You're the complete package." I kiss him fully, willing my lips to show him just how much he means to me.

He breaks the kiss and gives me a serious look, with a glint of mischief in his eyes.

"Callie."

"Yes, Gabe."

"Did you know you sound like a chipmunk when you sleep?"

"What? No!" I exclaim in shock, laughing.

"You do. You were making these little squeaks on and off throughout the night."

I tickle him playfully. "You're just messing with me again."

"No! You do, it's like this." He makes a high pitched chip, chip, chip.

"Well, I guess my dirty secret is out: I'm part chipmunk. Will you still have me?"

"Have you? I'm a lost cause. You could pretty much do anything now. I'm a goner, hook, line, and sinker."

I feel my stomach flip and heat spread throughout my body at his confession. I am so choked up, I can't respond, but my not-so-romantic stomach decides to rear its ugly head again and grumbles even louder.

He smiles broadly. "Alright, I can't take it. We have to feed you. I can't have my woman starving."

He called me his woman.

And then he kisses me, reminding me just how blessed I am to be here with this wonderful man. I feel dizzy. Is it the passion? Is it because I am starving? It doesn't matter. I choose Gabe. Over and over again, I'd choose Gabe. Food and my stupid stomach can wait. I'm going to savor this moment.

"How about a little more dessert first?" I murmur, trailing kisses down his neck, "and then I'll let my man get me some breakfast."

WE ARE SMILING like fools when we step outside the cabin. The stark, bright glare from all the snow piles around us is jarring. We both recoil a bit, squinting. Gabe mimes being blind.

"If we didn't need sustenance, I'd be scooping you up and carrying you back inside."

"You still can. Just feed me first."

"Deal." He winks at me and then reaches over and takes my hand in his as we walk towards the main lodge.

The simple act of holding his hand gives me goosebumps all over.

I feel like I am going to explode with happiness.

I called and spoke with my grandma last night and she said that she was watching Christmas movies with Jules and she was going to spend the night. She assured me they were having a wonderful time and, when I said I might try to make it home, she insisted that I don't hurry back.

I am about to text Jules, asking her how things are going when I see she has already messaged saying she is still at our apartment. I love how close she is with my grandma, and I am relieved she wasn't alone last night.

Gabe and I are both starving, so we decide to have breakfast here. We hurry our way inside, shivering from the icy air that assaults us on the short walk over. As soon as the door shuts behind us, we are greeted by a loud peal of laughter and excited conversation coming from the meeting room off the lobby.

"Sounds like we're crashing an event. Do you want to go somewhere else?" He looks at me, curious.

I decode the real question underneath: do you want people to know about us? It had crossed my mind that having breakfast in the morning in front of Doris is akin to announcing to all of Hopemeadow that we are a couple, but I don't care. I want the world to know that he is mine. And now, with whatever function is going on here, that seems to be a certainty.

"No, this is perfect." I give his hand a squeeze. He cocks his head to the side and gives me a lopsided grin, the laugh lines around his eyes wrinkling.

"Alright. Let's do this."

We walk into the meeting room, hands linked, and find 15 of the old ladies from town dressed head to toe in Christmas apparel. The room has four large round tables in the center, all decorated with festive tablecloths and poinsettias. There is a large breakfast buffet in the corner, and a piano on the opposite side of the room that is covered with various small presents and gift bags. A banner across the back wall reads, "Happy Holidays, Hopemeadow Knitters."

I whisper to Gabe, "I think we're crashing the knitting club holiday party."

He whispers back. "These ladies know what's up. Look at that spread. French toast? Piles of bacon? Cinnamon buns? I'll learn to knit to get in on this action each year."

I try to hold back a laugh and instead snort loudly, announcing our presence to the room. Everyone turns to look at us.

Nothing like making an embarrassing entrance.

There is a low hum as the ladies begin talking quietly to one another, clearly commenting on us.

Doris makes a beeline straight towards us.

"Callie! Gabe! I take it you both had a relaxing evening?" Her eyes glitter and she purses her lips as she eyes our hands, trying to contain her excitement. It is cute how happy she is for us.

"Yes, thank you. It was lovely. It's been a while since I've been inside the cabins. They are so cozy. Thanks again for letting me crash here."

"I can whip you up something in the dining room or you're welcome to join us here! There's plenty of food and cheer to go around!"

"We wouldn't want to impose…"

"No imposition at all!" Doris turns to the other ladies. "Ladies!! Callie and Gabe will be joining us this morning!" A ripple of hellos and easy smiles spreads through the room.

We help ourselves to the buffet and find our way over to a few empty seats near Doris. Wilma, Dorothy, and Bea sit with her and have already finished their breakfast. We make our introductions and then we sit down to eat.

Wilma is the first to start the inquisition that I know is coming.

I give them five minutes before it gets personal and they ask about us.

"Gabe, how are you enjoying Hopemeadow so far?" she says.

"It's been great. Such a beautiful town. Glad I was able to experience the holiday season. Callie has been showing me around and I'm thoroughly impressed."

"It is a wonderful town. Lived here my whole life. Do you think you'll be visiting again?"

His blue eyes glint at me. "Absolutely."

My heart flutters with excitement and longing, realizing I don't want him to just visit.

I want him to stay.

Bea jumps in. "I heard you were selling your property next to Honey's. There was a nasty rumor Bon Bon's was going to try to get their hands on it. That can't be true, right?"

Gabe reassures them. "No, I won't be selling to them. No need to worry."

The ladies all exchange knowing glances and smiles.

I take a bite of my French toast just as Dorothy decides to put it all out on the table. "So, what's going on here between you two? Is this just a holiday fling or are you two serious?"

I choke and cough on my food, eyes watering.

Dang, Dorothy. I haven't even asked that one yet!

Gabe takes the question in stride, as if it isn't intrusive or at all inappropriate. "You can't have a fling with a woman like this. She's one of a kind." He grabs my hand and brings it up to his lips, kissing it lightly.

I press my lips together tightly to stop myself from smiling too much. But I can't contain it. I beam with joy.

We finish up our breakfast and the rest of the conversation turns to what a wonderful job Doris did pulling together this party. Doris demurs, bemoaning the failure of her overhead speakers and the lack of holiday music.

"No music? Well, we can't have that." Gabe gets up and walks over to the piano. I watch him in awe as he sits down and rolls his shirt sleeves up tight, just to the edge of his elbow, his forearms strong and poised near the keys. "I'm taking requests!"

Doris claps her hands in glee as a handful of women start to gather around the piano. "Ah, you're a pianist! How marvelous! How about 'We Wish You a Merry Christmas?'"

"You got it."

I watch in wonder as he begins to play, enchanted by the

sight of his fingers moving skillfully over the keys. I had no idea he knew how to play piano and with such skill. A few of the ladies start to sing along.

He fits right in. Everyone loves him. I do my best to keep my eyes from prickling with tears.

Doris comes over and stands by my side. She wraps her arm around my waist and says, "This is one of the good ones, honey. Don't let him go."

CHAPTER 22

GABE

I PULL UP TO J&M CONSTRUCTION AND TURN OFF THE ENGINE. Today is the day I start to put my plan into action. Callie doesn't know it yet, but I am all in. I spent yesterday evening reading through her business proposal, and it is brilliant. In that proposal, she outlines a scenario where I would be a silent partner, but I have come up with something even better. A way to make everything we both want come true.

Instead of being a silent partner, I am excited at the prospect of joining forces and creating something new. Together. We can merge our backgrounds and offer something unique to Hopemeadow: a combined bakery and wine bar that would appeal to an even broader customer base. With my experience and connections to the wine industry, I can bring West Coast wines to the East Coast. We can build the bar, the stage area that Callie was hoping for, and add a nightlife element. The additional space will still allow for the extra commercial appliances and room she needs to expand for wholesaling her products.

I am excited, but I want to understand what a renovation this size would look like and dig deeper into the financials to make sure I can bring an equal backing to the table. I can't wait to surprise her and know that it will all fall into place. But first I need to pull it together and make sure it is doable.

I already spoke with Abby and asked her to take down the listing for the building. Now I need to find the right company to help me understand the renovations and get some ballpark numbers. This morning when I left the inn, Doris suggested I get in touch with J&M. She seemed reluctant to refer me to them, but said they are the best in town.

I walk into the small lobby and there is no one at the front desk.

"Hello?" I call out toward the back to see if anyone is around.

I am about to leave when I hear a man behind me say, "Twice in one week. To what do I owe the honor?"

I turn around. It is Jake, the man Callie had been fighting with at the ice skating rink. He is smiling, but the smile doesn't reach his eyes. His posture is rigid, his arms crossed.

"I don't think we've officially met. I'm Gabe Montgomery."

"Jake Anderson. Did you come here to see me?" His jaw is set as he eyes me suspiciously.

"No. Doris Winkleblack highly recommended J&M. Is this your business? I was looking to sit down with someone to talk about a renovation project."

"The owners, John and Mike, aren't here. They are the ones you'd want to sit down with to discuss the scope of the job." His eyes narrow, then he nonchalantly adds, "But I'd be more than happy to discuss it with you and get down some initial details."

Jake waves me back and points to a seat at a conference table tucked back in the corner of the office.

Everything about him rubs me the wrong way. I hate the way he walks and the smug tone of his voice. Even the way he gestures coolly to me to sit seems arrogant and dismissive.

If I were being honest with myself, I'd admit the reason I

disliked him is only because I know there is some history between him and Callie. She didn't tell me much, other than the fact that he isn't her boyfriend. But when he saw us holding hands, he certainly reacted like he has a claim on her.

Either way, I don't like it.

I debate leaving. I have no desire to work with a guy who has a thing for Callie. But part of me is curious to stick around and attempt to discover just how much of it lingers.

Jake opens a notepad. "So tell me a bit about this project."

"I'm the owner of the empty building next to Honey's, where Lou's Trinkets and Treasures used to be."

He eyes me coolly. "Yes, I'm aware. Callie has big hopes for your building."

"I see." Thrown, I pause. "Did she tell you that?"

What type of relationship do these two have? How does he know Callie's hopes for the future?

"Yes. She has been drafting a business proposal for a while." He presses on. "What are you intending to do with the building? Did you two come to an agreement?"

"I'm sorry, but what exactly did Callie tell you? I just want to make sure this isn't a conflict of interest."

He leans back in his chair and folds his arms. "You two have been spending a lot of time together lately, haven't you?"

My annoyance flares, but I try to stifle it so it doesn't show on my face. "I'm not sure how that's relevant to the project."

His lips curl into a smile. "It's not a conflict of interest. I don't see you as a threat."

I clench my teeth and stand to leave. "Ok, I get it. I'll find another company."

"No, I didn't mean that negatively. Have a seat. That came out the wrong way." He seems conciliatory, but something about the way he says it feels insincere.

"Look, I know we just met and all, but you know Callie. I'm

sure she mentioned that we have been having problems lately. She got upset while we were in Jamaica and..."

I stop him, taken aback. "You were in Jamaica together?"

"Yeah, I surprised her with a romantic getaway. We had been so excited about it, but you know how things can go in relationships with misunderstandings and whatnot. She gets so stressed out over Honey's. I just wanted her to get away and not think about work for a while."

"I see." I am completely blindsided, and "I see" seems to be the only response I have in me.

"Anyway, I don't need to bore you with the details, but I can promise you there won't be an issue here at J&M if you decide to hire us for the renovation. I keep business and my relationships separate." He gives me a knowing smile.

It takes everything in me to not leap across the table and punch him in the face.

I simply say, "Right."

"And sorry for acting like a possessive jerk at the rink. I get protective. I knew she was working on securing a deal with you, so I promised myself I'd give her space to wrap that up, let you two spend some time talking business, and we could reconnect after. But seeing that you're here, it looks like things went well. I'll have to send her flowers to congratulate her."

That is about all I can stand to hear.

"I think there's been a misunderstanding." I stand to leave and start towards the door.

Jake stands, too. "Oh. Are you not going into business with her? Was this to look into renovations for another plan you're considering?"

I stop, turn around, and stare at him, not responding.

"I'm sorry, man. I thought you knew about us. She probably was just trying to keep her personal life private until she signs the deal. She'll do whatever it takes for that bakery, you know?"

"It's not a problem. I'll call and set up an appointment for another day. Thanks for your time."

"Sure, I'll let John and Mike know to keep an eye out for your call."

I slam the door behind me, the crushing cold air hitting me like a wall.

Maybe I don't know as much about Callie as I thought.

CHAPTER 23

CALLIE

"Thanks for making the drop with me, Cam," I say, out of breath from running back and forth.

Cameron and I just returned to the bakery after dropping off the materials I donated for the cookie decorating event at the children's department in the library. Each year kids register early and spend hours perfecting their creations so Honey's can display them in the store for customers to vote on. The child who receives the most votes wins a free treat a week for a year. It's a highly coveted prize by the 10-and-under crowd and is always a fun event to sponsor.

It also brings quite a bit of foot traffic into the shop so everyone can see the final entries and they always end up buying something. It is a win-win all around.

"Well, you do pay me. Not sure if I had much of a choice," she says sarcastically as she starts flouring the counter to roll out some dough.

"Watch it, lady, or that check might be short this week," I tease. Cameron tosses a little flour at me and I dodge out of the way.

"Speaking of money and becoming destitute, am I still going

to have a job next year? Have you heard anything else about the sale next door? Is Bon Bon's moving in?"

"Dang, you cut right to the chase, don't you?" Typical Cam. She never beats around the bush. She has always been highly sarcastic and generally hot-tempered, but I know I can always count on her to be straight with me. I love that no-nonsense side of her.

"You'll be happy to know that Gabe promised I don't have to worry about Bon Bon's. He won't be selling to them."

"Hey! That's freaking wonderful! Not for nothing, but I can't believe that idiot was actually going to sell to them. Who does that?" Cam is loyal to a fault and is like a rabid dog if people go after the ones she loves. It's usually a verbal take down, but it's powerful, nonetheless. I've always said I'm glad I'm her friend and not her enemy.

"Hey now, he's not so bad," I say.

She looks at me, doubtful. "First he is the enemy coming in to crush all your hopes and dreams, and now he's not so bad? What am I missing? Did he look over your proposal for the expansion and decide to go in on it with you?"

"Um, no."

"Then I'm definitely missing something."

I hesitate. "He looked over the proposal, or he says he did, but he's still going to sell the building. It's the right thing for him to do."

Cameron shifts to the side and purses her lips. She doesn't like big displays of emotion, but by the tight look on her face, I can tell she feels bad for me.

She says, "Ok, so you know I'm not one of those girls who hugs, right? Like, the thought of hugging you right now makes me cringe… but I feel like this is one of those moments I *should* hug you…" She slowly starts to open her arms and moves toward me, but looks as if she is about to scald herself against a hot stove.

The lame attempt to hug me is incredibly sweet coming from her.

I laugh and push her away. "Stoppp." She looks instantly relieved. "I'm fine. Really, it's fine."

"Is it? Can you tell me you're fine one more time? I think three fines in a row should convince me you really mean it."

I roll my eyes. "I've made peace with it. I can find other ways to expand Honey's down the road. Maybe I could even buy a second food truck or something."

"You've had your heart set on this for so long. Why are you suddenly so ok with this and willing to give up?"

How can I explain this to her in a way she will understand? I know how it makes me look. "I don't know… I just want him to be happy."

Cameron recoils and puts her hands on her hips. "Ok, what in the world happened? Is he dying? Are you dying? Is the place secretly infested with rodents and now you don't want it?"

I burst out laughing. "Everyone is healthy! Why would you even say that?"

"Because I know you and I know you've *always* wanted this. Then at the drop of a dime, this guy shows up and suddenly you're 'just *fine*' with letting it all go? What's gotten into you?"

"We've gotten close. It's different now."

"What's different?" Her eyes grow wide. "Wait, are you two together?"

"Well… I'm not exactly sure what we are, but yes, something's happening. He's wonderful, Cam. He's different from the other guys I've met before."

I'm expecting her to be happy for me, but instead she shakes her head. She looks disappointed. "Oh boy, here we go."

"What is that supposed to mean?"

She stares at me with a no nonsense expression. "Don't make me say it."

"Well, it sounds like you already have a burning desire to say something, so spit it out." I know Cam and I brace myself.

"You do this. This is your self-sabotage move."

"What are you talking about?"

"You meet a guy and, when you fall for the guy, you try to change to make him happy. Or you get distracted, and things at Honey's start to slide. You're a powerhouse, Callie, but when it comes to men, they're your weakness every time. It's like you put blinders on and you don't see what's happening until it's too late."

I head over to the display case and start wiping it down in a lame attempt at distraction. For some reason, I don't want to look her in the eye. "Down, girl. It's getting brutal in here."

"I'm not saying this to be mean," she says sincerely, "but you need to stop thinking with your lady bits."

I laugh and emphatically shook my head no. "That's so not true! Sure, I admit I don't always have the best taste in guys, but Honey's is always my number one priority!"

"I know you want it to be, but these guys mess with your head and you end up making bad choices. Do you remember when you almost gave up the food truck for Ray? Mr. Insecure didn't like you running it and said it was getting in the way of your time together. You were so close to selling it, all because he was the first guy to say he loves you."

Ok, that was true. My ex-boyfriend Ray complained that I had no time for him and was jealous of the truck. He was also an emotional terrorist who had a way of always making me feel inadequate. I start in on my rebuttal, but she just keeps going, talking over me.

"Jake was the same. He was getting in the way of Honey's all the time. Seriously, it's like all these guys are threatened by a strong woman and have an issue with you owning this business. It's like they think it makes them less of a man if you are more successful than they are."

Hearing her lay it out like this has me wondering if there is some truth to it.

"Think about it, Callie. Why would Jake go out of his way to convince you to go on a trip during your busiest season, when you would never want to do that? Then after you go, you find out the selfish jerk made you pay for all of it and had planned activities you would never want to do! That's all sabotage. None of these guys can handle you being successful. Are you sure that isn't happening here, too?"

"No! Gabe never said either way what he wanted to do with Honey's. I didn't give him a chance. I was the one who told him he should sell. This was my idea. He's supportive of my business."

"Then he did some Jedi mind trick crap on you."

"Cam…"

"SAB-O-TAGE," she says, over enunciating each syllable.

"Cam, I know you're trying to help, but you've got this one wrong."

"I just want you to be careful, Callie. You have a blind spot when it comes to relationships."

I am saved by the bell when Gina Gillroy comes in and stands at the counter. Gina has three kids and somehow always looks pulled together and in control. I don't know how she does it. She is that perfect mom that makes you wonder if things are really as perfect as they look on the outside.

"We'll finish this later," I say to Cameron on my way up to the front.

"Hi Gina! How's it going? How are the kids?"

"Hi! Everyone's great. Just stopping by for some after dinner treats for the kids. Can I get two of those cookies and two slices of the chocolate torte for Ted and I? Oh, and throw in a blueberry muffin for me. I'll eat it here in peace before I go grab the kids from school."

"Ok, so the two slices of torte and three... wait, did you say only two cookies? Is one of the kids out tonight?"

"Yes, just two cookies. Billy got in trouble for using a cuss word in school again today." She rolls her eyes as she pays.

I chuckle and she heads over to the café to sit down to eat.

Cameron comes up from the back and brings with her another tray of pastries for the display case.

"Look, I'm sorry if I overstepped. I get worried about you sometimes. But you do seem pretty good since you've been back from Jamaica, all things considered. With all that's been happening, if I were you, I'd probably be rocking in a corner somewhere stuffing my face full of pie and chugging a bottle of vodka."

I smile. "I'm doing good. I've got this all under control. Gabe isn't pulling anything and I'm right on track here."

Gina walks back up with a disgusted look on her face.

That's not a look you ever want to see on one of your customers. "Gina, are you ok? What's wrong?"

"Callie, I don't mean to be rude, but this muffin tastes... well, it's not your usual."

"What do you mean?"

"Why don't you taste one?"

I grab a piece of wax paper, pick up a muffin from the glass case, and take a bite.

Ugh! This is disgusting! What did I do??

I spit it out into a napkin. All I can taste is salt. I *always* try a small taste of each item before putting it out. I must have been so distracted this morning my quality control slipped. The only thing I can think of is that I used salt in place of sugar when I was making the batter.

Cam stares at me and I can almost hear her saying *I told you so* with her eyes.

I toss the remaining tray of muffins in the trash and wonder if maybe Cam is right.

But I am the common denominator here.

It isn't just the guys. It is me. I lose focus and let them sway me. I need to stay in control and not let myself get distracted from what's really important.

I can't make that mistake again, and certainly not with Gabe.

CHAPTER 24

CALLIE

"Wait, I'm not following. He did what?"

"I'm sorry, Mr. Montgomery said that you two were about to go into business together and are renovating the space next door. He was looking into the necessary building permits, and he left behind some forms. It's a lot of bureaucracy and J&M should take care of most of that for you, but we're so happy to hear that Honey's is going to be expanding!"

Renovations? J&M? Permits?

I try to stay calm and not let on that all of this is news to me. "Thanks so much for touching base, Brad. If you could just email me exactly what you need and send over the forms, I'll be sure to look them over."

"Great. I'll get them to you soon. Thanks, Callie and congrats again!"

I hang up the phone, shaking in anger. I sit down at my desk and put my head in my hands.

This is my business, and somehow Gabe is taking over and planning things without consulting with me first? Last I knew, we agreed he was selling the building. We haven't even discussed my business proposal, and now he's working on a renovation plan *without me.*

There is a knock at my office door and I look up to find Jake standing there, looking hesitant. "Hey Callie, I hope I'm not interrupting you."

Not this guy again. I cannot handle this right now.

Anger is laced through my voice as I say, "What are you doing here? Who let you back here?"

I am expecting another fight, but immediately I can see that Jake seems skittish, almost nervous. "I came in through the back. I wanted to talk to you about something important and I knew if I called, you wouldn't pick up."

"I already told you. I have nothing to say to you."

"It's about Gabe."

I go still and my tone grows cold. "What about him? What, you didn't screw me over enough while we were in Jamaica, so now you're trying to mess with me and Gabe?"

"I have no idea what you're talking about, but I do think he is up to something. That's why I came here. I need to know. What did you two agree on?"

I busy myself with papers on my desk. "None of this is any of your business."

He softens his voice and says, "I'm just looking out for you… as a friend."

I laugh bitterly. "You're *not* my friend."

"How can you be so distant and just turn it all off like that?" He moves closer to me as I stand up from the desk. "I said a lot of awful things last time I was here. I was hurt, and I wanted to hurt you back. I'm sorry." He inches a bit closer and his voice falls deep. "Do you remember how we used to be together? How things were when it was just you and me? We had a lot of fun."

"Don't! I don't have time for this nonsense anymore. How can you even say that with a straight face after what you did? We are not together. It's over."

"I don't know why you're so angry with me, but I need you to hear me when I say Gabe is moving in on your business. There's no way you would let him come in to discuss renovations for Honey's without you there. Unless you've decided to just let him take over."

"Not that I believe you, but you're claiming he talked to you about renovations for Honey's?"

"Yes. He came in saying he had a large scale renovation project that he was going to be undertaking. He was acting shifty. I couldn't tell if he was pulling something on you or if he was moving forward with the deal with Bon Bon's. Did you two agree to go into business together?"

I pause and then admit the truth. "No."

"Is he selling to Bon Bon's then?" he asks.

"He said he wasn't."

"I hate to be the one to tell you this, but no matter what way you spin this, Gabe isn't the guy you think he is. I think he could tell I was getting suspicious, so he left and didn't want to talk to me about the project anymore. John said they are supposed to meet tomorrow to discuss the job."

I walk out of my office and out the back door into the parking lot. I'm not wearing a coat, and it is freezing. The sky is gray, and the wind feels harsh against my face. I don't care if it's cold and that it stings. I need to feel anything for a moment that isn't this sinking feeling of betrayal.

I can't believe Gabe would do this. I don't know who I can trust anymore.

Jake follows me out, but keeps his distance.

"I'm sorry I upset you. Really, I am. I just want to help. I know I've been terrible lately and you deserve better. I know that now. And when it comes to us? I got jealous, ok? It's hard to watch you with Honey's. I can't keep up with you. When we were together, you're all anyone wanted to talk about. It was never about me or what I was doing. It was always, how's

Callie? How's Honey's? Isn't she amazing? And yeah, I agree, you're amazing, but I felt like a shadow with you. No one ever saw *me* anymore. Not even you."

I stare at him as the snow begins to fall. I have never heard him say anything like this before. I had no idea he felt this way.

I blink, almost at a loss for words. "I'm sorry, I didn't know."

"I know. I never said anything because it's an awful thing to admit. I'm not proud of it. But I am happy for you. I want you to do well. I just didn't know where I fit into all of that."

I stand there silent for a moment, taking it all in. "Thank you for telling me."

He nods and takes off his coat. He walks toward me, slowly, like he is afraid I am about to run away. "Take my coat, ok? You look like you're freezing."

I feel numb. I let him drape it over my shoulders.

"I'm going to head out. I'm sorry for getting you so upset. That's the last thing I want."

He starts to walk off towards his truck when I call out to him.

"Jake!" He turns to face me. "Tell me the truth. Do you think Gabe is trying to manipulate me?"

"He's definitely planning something. Don't let him play you, Callie. You should be treated like a queen. I just hope to become the kind of guy who deserves a woman like you someday."

I can't believe it. Cameron is right about everything.

It's happening again. I'm messing everything up because I let these guys get into my heart and head. I have to protect myself.

I have to break it off with Gabe for good.

CHAPTER 25

GABE

"This is it," Abby says, pushing the door open and backing up so I can enter. I walk inside the empty apartment on the second floor and look around.

I thank Abby for letting me in, and she shows me how to use the lockbox outside to secure the building when I am done. I thank her and go inside alone.

It is a large open, two-bedroom with 20th century charm and worn, original hardwood floors throughout. French doors lead into a large dining room and living room that highlight a brick fireplace. Natural light streams in through oversized accent windows, and the crown molding and built in cabinetry give the apartment a vintage feel. Although it clearly needs work, the kitchen is bright and has a unique mosaic tile backsplash with a walk-in pantry.

The best part of the apartment is the private balcony off the master bedroom. The view from the back overlooks the valley and you can see the city in the distance.

Everything about it has an old school allure, and with some contemporary renovations, a coat of paint, and high-end upgrades of the appliances, the apartment could be incredible.

No one has lived here since my grandfather left all those years ago. He had it cleaned once every few years, but insisted on keeping it empty. I never understood why he didn't want to rent this space along with the first floor below, but after talking to Alice, I have a feeling I now know why.

A few pieces of furniture remain: an old kitchen table, a bookshelf in the living room, and an antique desk and chair in the master bedroom. There are two books left behind, *Pride & Prejudice* and *Wuthering Heights*. I pick them up to take home with me. I haven't read either, but I think my mother might like them knowing they were my grandfather's.

I run my fingers along the desk in the bedroom and sit in the chair. I imagine my grandfather here, and my heart feels heavy, knowing he has been here once, and now he is gone.

I pull on a drawer and it sticks with age. I give it another hard yank, and it begrudgingly releases. I rifle through the papers inside, excited to see they are his. There are a few formal college essays for a business class and utility bills from his stay. As I am reading, I hear Abby call out to me.

"Gabe, are you still here?"

"Yes, I was just looking at some papers in the desk here. It's like a time capsule."

Abbey stands in the doorway to the bedroom. "Ah, good, I'm glad. I'm sorry to interrupt, but a representative from Bon Bon's called and increased their offer. Are you certain you are not interested in selling? It is likely the best offer you will get considering other comparable buildings, and it's well above asking."

I shake my head, dismissing the idea. "No, I can't do it."

"Are you sure? The only other interested party indicated they would want concessions based on some of the expected electrical and plumbing issues they noticed during their walk through. Bon Bon's would be the smart choice."

She's right. Financially, it would be the smart choice. But I could never do anything to hurt Callie. It's a done deal now. I can't sell to Bon Bon's.

"I'm aware. But I've decided to keep the building. Should anything change down the road, I still wouldn't feel good selling to them based on what I know about the business next door."

"As your realtor, I need to let you know that is a mistake financially, but I understand your decision."

I thank her for her help, grab the papers from the drawer, and tuck the books under my arm. As I am about to leave, I glance out the kitchen window and see Jake's truck leaving Honey's parking lot. Confused, I walk closer to the window and see Callie walking back into the bakery with his jacket around her shoulders, looking upset.

I feel my jaw clench. When I left J&M, I tried not to let what Jake said get in my head, but seeing this makes me question everything. Everything in me screams that Callie would never use me to get access to this property, but is there still something going on with her and Jake? I'm not going to wonder and wait anymore. I can't allow this to be a miscommunication. It's time to find out.

I walk outside and enter through the back door of Honey's. I find Callie alone, her face tear stained and red, staring off at the wall. I know I should ask if she is ok, but seeing her in his coat enrages me all over again.

I stop in the doorway of her office, my stomach churning. "We need to talk."

She looks at me, her eyes blank, unfeeling. My heart sinks and throat clenches.

I can tell by her face everything is different.

She says, "Yes, we do."

There's no point in delaying this any longer. I can hardly move as I ask, "What's going on with you and Jake?"

She looks at me baffled, but numb. "Why are you asking me this?"

"I saw him leaving Honey's and here you are wearing his coat."

Her face burns red. "Are you spying on me?"

What kind of answer is that? Why is she being like this?

"Answer the question, Callie."

She squares her shoulders. "I don't owe you any explanation."

"Why didn't you tell me you were with him in Jamaica?"

She looks surprised that I know this, but makes no apologies. "It never came up."

"I asked you at the airport if you had a boyfriend and you said no. Why are you keeping all this from me?"

Sadness tears at my chest and I feel my eyes start to well with emotion. I rein it in, doing my best to stay in control.

"This has nothing to do with you. You don't have the right to grill me. You have no claim on me. You're not my boyfriend."

It feels like a kick to the gut. "No claim on you? Is that what you think I'm trying to do? Callie, all I want is to be close to you. Why do you keep pushing me away? Why can't you just trust me and let me in?"

"Because there is no way this could ever work. We've been avoiding the inevitable."

"So that's it? You just decide all of this in your head and that's that? No conversation, no attempt to work it out, we're just done?"

"Yes. I'm sorry, but whatever we were doing is over."

My voice rises, incredulous. "How can you do that?"

"How can you go behind my back and start moving in on my business without talking to me first?"

I falter, taken aback by the question. "What? Are you serious?"

"What are you trying to do, Gabe? Is your plan to agree to be a silent partner and then eventually push me out? We hadn't even talked about my business proposal once and suddenly I hear you're over at J&M talking design plans without me?"

"I was going to surprise you! I know how much you want this expansion. I had it all planned. I was going to get the drawings, figure out the specifics, and then bring it to you. I would never try to move forward in any way with Honey's without you. I was trying to help."

"Wait. What big plan? I already gave you my business proposal, outlined in detail."

I shake my head, hating that my plan to surprise her is being misunderstood. "This isn't the way I wanted to discuss it."

"Well, now you have to. Tell me. What's your plan?"

I sigh, frustrated. "Can we just take a step back and talk about this later? You're upset, I'm upset. I feel like this is going south, fast."

"No. I want you to tell me."

"I was going to suggest that we combine our passions and turn Honey's into a combined bakery and wine bar. With my knowledge of wine and connections to the business, we could put Honey's on the map. We could align ourselves with the Connecticut wine trail. It would still allow you to expand in all the ways you wanted, but I'd be able to forge ahead with my dream, too. We'd have it all."

"Are you insane? You can't just plan our entire life without talking to me first. And does this mean you're planning on staying in Hopemeadow? Suddenly you've decided you want in on Honey's, plan to completely change my business, and I'm just finding out about it now. Until now, I was still thinking you were leaving for California soon."

I never looked at it that way. From her perspective, I can see why she would be concerned, but does she really think I'd do anything that would hurt her?

"I get it. This is overwhelming. This is not the way I wanted any of this to go down. I can see why this looks bad and that it's moving too fast for you, but we really could have it all. We both could get everything we ever wanted. We could do it and be together."

I reach out to take her hand, and she pushes it away. "Maybe in your eyes. You can't just make decisions like that without talking to me. You can't steamroll me with my own business! This is *my* life. *My* business. I say what happens here, not you."

"So I'm the bad guy for being romantic?"

"No, you're the bad guy for assuming I would just be so thrilled that you want to become a part of my life and business that I'd drop everything I had planned and let you change all of it without my say. I won't change for you. I've been down that road. I'm not doing it again." She crosses her arms and turns away from me.

"Your way or the highway, right, Callie? You could never be wrong. There is no compromise. This is your truth and there can't possibly be another way but yours?"

"Don't make this harder than it needs to be. I gave you your out. Sell the building. Leave. Do us both a favor before we get so far into this we can't find our way out."

My heart wrenches as my hope turns to despair. She's ending this. I can't believe she's ending this.

I've never felt this way before about another woman. She's everything to me and now she is ending it all for no reason.

My voice cracks with emotion. "I don't want to find my way out. I love you, Callie."

She looks terrified and backs away. She whispers, "What did you just say?"

I double down and say the words I've been wanting to say for days. "I said I love you. I don't want to leave. I want to stay in Hopemeadow. Please tell me you feel the same and you want nothing to do with Jake anymore."

A tear falls down her face and she says, "I can't do that…"

I stand still. "Are you saying there is something still going on with you and Jake?"

"Gabe, I..."

I shake my head in denial. This cannot be happening. "I don't believe you. You're lying to push me away. You wouldn't do that."

"I have to go. I can't do this." She runs out, leaving me standing there wondering how everything went so wrong, so fast.

So much for grand gestures.

CHAPTER 26

CALLIE

"STOP CRYING, TAKE A BREATH. WHAT'S GOING ON?" JULES LOOKS at me, concerned. "Come here." She wraps me in her arms in a hug and rubs my back. "You're scaring me. I've never seen you this upset before."

After the fight with Gabe, I ran to her apartment down the street. I didn't know where else to go. I don't want my grandma to see me like this and get worried. Sniffling, I try to get my breathing under control.

"Jules, it was awful," I say, sobbing.

"What was awful?"

"Gabe. I should have never trusted him. I had blinders on again, just like Cam said."

"Like Cam said?" Jules makes a face like she smells something bad. "You're taking relationship advice from Cam? Don't do that. We've seen her in action and that is its own train wreck. I love her, but that girl has trust issues."

"It doesn't matter. She was right. He was planning on trying to take over Honey's the whole time, and I was too dumb to see it."

"How could he take over Honey's? Did he lie about selling to Bon Bon's?"

"No, this has nothing to do with Bon Bon's. He went behind my back and started coming up with plans to turn Honey's into a joint bakery and wine bar."

Jules hesitates and then grins. "That actually sounds like a great idea. And with his background…"

"You're not listening. He went to J&M and was talking to John about renovation plans *without me*. He's trying to take over. He doesn't want to be a silent partner. He wants an equal say."

Jules nods and appears to be taking a minute to consider how to respond. "Callie, I know you're upset, and I am sensitive to that, but is it possible you're jumping to conclusions?"

"He thinks he can just come in here and tell me how to run my business! He's not going to manipulate me or get me distracted so he can swoop in. I worked too hard to let that happen."

Jules looks at me wide eyed. "Callie, I know you've been hurt. You've fought for this business and there have been guys who have been intimidated along the way. But I really don't think Gabe is that guy. You're making all these assumptions. Did you talk to him about it?"

I sniff and slowly say, "Yes and no."

"What does that mean?"

"He told me the plan and then he was saying all these crazy things."

"What crazy things?"

I whisper, "He said I love you and that he wanted to move here."

"That cad! What a jerk! How can you ever forgive him!" she says sarcastically.

"Jules! I'm serious!"

"I am, too! How dare he say he loves you and basically that

he wants to spend his whole life with you! I would run, too. The last thing you need is a guy who is secure and committed to you." She looks at me with a face that says, *are you insane?*

"This is all moving too fast. Every time I fall for a guy I make terrible decisions, especially with Honey's."

"That's not true. Don't let the dumb stuff Cam says get in your head. Yes, you've had bad relationships. And yes, there have been guys that have tried to get in the way, but the keyword is tried. You never let that happen. Don't let the past dictate your future, Callie. You can't just judge people and run away without giving them a chance. You have to talk. Not everyone is out to get you. It's ok to be vulnerable and to trust people."

I drop my head in my hands. "I'm just so afraid."

"What is there to be afraid of? From what I can tell, it sounds like he decided to change his own dreams for you. He had a plan before he met you and now he is going to uproot his entire life. *For you.* That doesn't happen every day, Callie. That is rare. That's the kind of thing you fight for, not against."

She's right. He's going out of his way to give up his future and being brave enough to envision a new one. One that includes me. I've been so guarded that I can't even see a good thing when it's right in front of me.

Gabe is the one. From the moment I've met him I've felt it deep in my soul.

It's like a weight has been lifted and the revelation fills me with joy.

I am head over heels, desperately and completely in love with Gabe.

"Oh my goodness, you're right. None of the rest of it matters, just like my grandma said! What am I doing?"

"It's ok! Just go talk to him."

"I might have made it sound like I was still into Jake to get him to leave me alone." I cringe.

Jules looks at me like I'm crazy. "Why would you do that?"

"Self-sabotage. Apparently, that's my thing, too." I rub my eyes and shake my head. "I just hope I can fix it before it's too late."

CHAPTER 27

I SIT IN MY CAR DEBATING WHAT TO DO. I DON'T WANT TO PUSH her, but we need to talk. I ruined everything. I was so confident she would love the idea that I violated her trust. I know she loves me too, and she is just scared to admit it. I came on too strong, too fast.

I get out of the car and head to her apartment. I have to make this right. I'll give her all the space she needs. I don't have to have anything to do with Honey's.

I just need her. That's all.

I knock on the door and when it opens, I feel physically sick.

It is Jake.

He says, "Hey, Gabe. Callie's not here."

I stand in the doorway in stunned silence. Jake is at her apartment answering her door.

That's all I need to know.

"Do you want me to call her for you? I think she should be home any time now, I..."

"No, that's ok." My heart feels like it is disintegrating into a million pieces. I turn to leave, and he stops me.

"You can wait here if you want. I talked to John earlier and I think I had the wrong idea about things with you and Honey's..."

I shake my head. I don't want to hear any more. I can't do this. "No, that's ok. I'm headed back to California a bit earlier than I expected. You don't have to tell her I stopped by."

"You sure? I..." he starts.

"Yeah, positive." I clench my jaw, willing myself to keep it together in front of him.

"Alright. Have a good flight."

"Thanks." My whole body reels in pain. I've lost the one woman I truly love. I have to get out of here.

Far away and never look back.

Before I turn to leave, I say, "And Jake? Take good care of her."

CHAPTER 28

CALLIE

"GRANDMA? I'M HOME!"

I come into the kitchen and toss my bag on the table. All I want to do is curl up in a ball in front of the Christmas tree, but I have to keep it together until I can find Gabe. I just need to check in on my grandma and then I can head to the inn.

As I round the corner, I'm stunned to see Jake. Jake in my apartment. Who does he think he is?

"Hey Callie, how's it going?"

This has to be a bad dream.

Annoyed, I say, "Jake, what are you doing here? Where's my grandma?"

"Shhh… keep your voice down. She's resting in her room. I swung by to grab my coat and she asked me to come in. She seemed lonely, so we played a hand of gin-rummy."

"Oh." I look at him, confused. "That was nice of you. Thanks."

"Yeah, that's what I thought, too. Man, you're quick to think the worst of me, aren't you?" He crosses his arms and glares at me, seeming more hurt than angry.

I mumble, "It's not like you won any boyfriend of the year awards."

"Was I really that bad? Sure, we are very different and probably should have broken up a while ago, but I didn't think you hated me."

I'm tired of dancing around the real issue. I have to call him out on what he did. After all this, he can't possibly think I don't know.

"Seriously?? Who asks a girl to go on a surprise vacation and then makes her pay for it? That was so shady, Jake. I was hoping to get through the holidays and then deal with you after, but I hope you plan on reimbursing me."

Jake's mouth drops and his eyes narrow. "That's a bad joke, right Cal?"

"Yeah, it *was* a bad joke. They rejected my card while we were in Jamaica. You're lucky I had another one on me so I could get home."

He clenches his jaw, furious. "Callie, I paid for that trip and I'm *still* paying it off."

"Spare me the lies. I'm over it now."

"I can't believe this." He sighs in frustration. "Yes, I put it on your card initially, but I paid it off the minute I got back. I had moved some money around from my savings account and I just figured it would be easier to put it all on your card and give you the reward points. Have you looked at your statement lately?"

I feel my face burn with embarrassment. "No, I haven't."

"I'd never steal from you, or anyone else for that matter." He looks insulted and hurt.

"I'm sorry. I just assumed..."

He cuts me off. "Yeah, you always 'just assume.'"

"Hey, wait a minute," I say angrily. "Yes, I could have stayed and talked to you, but when I went to the bar, you were dancing with some girl. It was insult after injury, so, yeah, of course I left."

"That woman you saw me dancing with had just been dumped and had been crying at the bar for hours. Her friends were trying to cheer her up, and they convinced me to dance with her. Yes, probably a terrible choice and I'm sure it looked bad, but I swear I didn't do anything with that woman. I went right back to my spot at the bar, had a few more drinks, and when I got back to the room you had disappeared."

This is all too much. I have to sit down.

"You do this all the time, you know. You make all these wild assumptions and insist you're right. No one has a chance. You make up your own story on what you want to believe about people."

I think back to everything that happened lately with Jake, Gabe at the airport, and with Honey's.

He is right. I have jumped to conclusions and hurt people along the way. I've been so blind. How did I not see this?

"I'm really sorry, Jake. You're right." I start to cry.

"Hey, hey, hey," Jake says in hushed tones, coming over to hug me. "Don't cry."

"Jake, I've screwed everything up. I ruined it all. I have no one to blame but myself."

He leans over to console me. "Hey, you and I both know we weren't going to make it. I'll always care about you, but you were right. We're just different people."

"I'm not talking about you!" I wail.

"Oh, ouch. Way to twist the knife." I see a flash of recognition in his eyes and then he says, "Gabe, right?"

"Yes. Gabe. I ruined it. I accused him of all sorts of terrible things, and I've been doing it from the minute we met."

"Look, you know I'm not a fan of that guy. He bothers me. His hair is too perfect, and he just looks smug, like he thinks he knows everything and... I mean, what type of man lets a penguin get the best of him?"

"Jake!" I cry.

"But… if he's the guy for you, you have to tell him."

"I don't even know what to say. How do I make this better now, after all I've done? Do I just show up at the inn and be like, 'Sorry I'm the worst, will you love me?'"

Jake grimaces. "Actually…"

Alarm bells go off in my mind by his tone. "Actually, what?"

"Well, he was here a few hours ago."

"WHAT?" My eyes grow wide. If he saw Jake here…

"He didn't say why he was here, but he might have gotten the wrong idea with me here. He said he was headed back to California and that I should take care of you."

"Why did you wait all this time to tell me that??" I practically yell.

Jake throws his arms up in protest. "Because you have been screaming at me or crying or accusing me of things non-stop since I got here."

Ugh! He's right. Again. This is a nightmare.

I scramble for my phone and try calling and texting Gabe. No response.

I lunge for my coat and keys on the counter. "I'm so sorry, but I have to go. I have to make this right."

"What are you going to do?"

"I don't know, but I have to at least try. I just hope I can catch him at the inn before he leaves."

If he heads to California without talking to me first, it could be the end of us. I have to stop him.

"You're a mess. You're going to get yourself killed. I'm driving you."

"Fine, but you better step on it!"

CHAPTER 29

CALLIE

Jake and I come to a screeching halt in front of the inn. I practically fall out of his truck, scrambling. I have no idea what I am going to say to him, but everything in me is screaming. I look around frantically for his rental car and am relieved to find it is still in front of his cabin. He hasn't left yet.

I take a deep breath and realize I am shaking.

He's the one. I can't lose him.

Jake follows me out of the car and I stop him.

"No, you can't be here. If he sees you, after everything that has happened, it wouldn't help."

He shakes his head in agreement. "You're right. Good luck, Callie. I hope you find what you're looking for."

I nod, swallowing down the rising fear of letting myself be vulnerable.

What if I've screwed this up so much he doesn't want me anymore?

The thought of losing him is too much for me to bear.

"And Callie?" he says.

"Yeah?"

"Don't let your pride get in the way. Just tell him how you feel."

"Since when did you become a love guru?" I say, chuckling.

"Since I screwed up yet another relationship. I might not be capable of having a decent relationship, but I know you can."

"Ok, I don't have time to talk you through that self-deprecating nonsense, but we will finish this conversation later!" I yell over my shoulder as I hurry inside.

I run into the lobby first, bursting in with a bit too much fanfare.

When I'm in panic mode, I tend to be a bit dramatic.

I'm working on it.

"My goodness, Callie! What has gotten into you? Are you ok?" Doris is at the front desk arranging a flower bouquet, staring at me confused.

I must look a mess.

I sit down in a giant wingback chair, wrap my arms around my body, and rock a bit.

I can't go charging in there like a crazy fool.

I. Must. Chill.

"Sorry, Doris, I'm in a bit of a crisis right now. I came to see Gabe. Just have to collect my thoughts for a moment."

"Ahh… going to tell him how you feel, eh?"

My eyes grow wide. "Excuse me?"

"Honey, I could have seen that coming from a mile away. That man is smitten with you, even from the beginning. The way you two looked at each other at the Hop was R rated and that was with you halfway to a concussion."

I burst out laughing. "Well, I'm glad everyone else could see it but me."

"What are you doing here? Go get that man. Here," she reaches behind the desk, fumbles for a moment, and then hands me something. "Bring this. It will help with the holiday spirit." She winks at me.

I look at what she handed me and a broad smile stretches across my face.

I walk outside and feel a flood of positivity. I just know this is all going to be okay. For once, I am going to make the right choice.

I round the building and his car is gone.

No!

I run to his door, and it is locked. I cup my hands up around my eyes and peer inside the window next to the door.

His suitcase is no longer there, and I don't see any of his things.

He is gone. He must have just left.

I turn around and start running to the parking lot and suddenly remember: I don't have a car here. Jake dropped me off.

I try to call Gabe again, and he sends me to voicemail.

Doris!

I rush back into the lobby and my face must say it all.

Doris clutches at her cardigan. "Oh goodness. What happened?"

Panicked, I say, "He left. He's headed back to California and I need your help. Can I borrow your car?"

She looks at me like I have three heads. "My *Corolla*? Oh no, dear. I've seen you drive."

I beg. "Please, Doris! I have to find him. He's not taking my calls. If he leaves, this could be it."

Doris sighs heavily. "I will drive you, but you are not taking my car."

I don't want to be ageist because I've honestly seen plenty of good, older people on the road, but Doris is the cliché old lady driver. She goes about 20 miles under the speed limit and I frequently see her driving over the lines on the road.

Not that I'm one to judge someone's driving, but at least I get places fast.

"You don't have to drive me! I have no idea if I will even find him or which airport he went to. He could be driving all the way to Boston for his flight, for all I know. Please, I will be so careful with your car! Plus, I'm sure you can't leave the inn unattended."

She thinks about it carefully, and all I can hear is the Jeopardy theme song music in my head as I wait for her to finally answer me.

"No."

She doesn't qualify it or make any excuses. Just no.

"Let me find my hat and gloves." She looks me over and her eyes land on my feet. "And be sure to wipe off your boots before you step in, Callie. I don't want any sludge getting in my Corolla."

Beggars can't be choosers.

AN HOUR LATER, we are approaching the exit for the airport and she drives right past it. It takes another half hour for her to find her way back and to get us to the terminal. Watching her try to find a place to park is torture, and I half contemplate jumping out of the car while it is still moving. I finally convince her to drop me off at the entrance so I can rush in to try to find him.

On the way to the airport, I find that there are two flights departing soon to California. I'm not sure if he is on either, but I have to at least try.

I feel like the protagonist in every cheesy romantic comedy out there, running through the airport, panicked, checking the departure times and rushing to the gate.

Except I'm not in a movie and this is real life. And in real life, they don't let you pass security to get to the gates, no matter how convincingly you plead.

I clearly haven't thought this through.

I plead with the balding, middle aged security guard in front of me. He does not look amused. "Sir, I swear, I just need to see if someone is at his gate!"

"I'm sorry, ma'am, if you're not a ticketed passenger you cannot go beyond this point."

I throw my hands up in frustration and then I see Gus.

Grumpy Gus!

I'm sure I have lost all credibility with him because of the luggage incident, but at least he knows what Gabe looks like.

I run over to him. "Gus! You have to help me!"

"I'm sorry, do I know you?" He puts his hand on his night-stick, on full alert.

"Yes! I'm the woman who accused that gorgeous tall man, Gabe Montgomery, of stealing my luggage! Do you remember me?"

He purses his lips, crosses his arms, and says dryly, "Right. How could I forget?"

"Well, you see, it's a crazy story, but, well, heck, I'll just say it. I ended up falling head over heels in love with that man and he is about to hop on a plane to California and I need to stop him."

The way he looks at me makes me feel two inches tall. "Let me get this straight; you accused him of being a thief and now you love him?"

I smile nervously. "Well... yes, that's the long and short of it."

"And how does this have anything to do with me?"

"I don't have a ticket and I don't have time to go through that whole crazy process. By the time I did, he would be gone. You remember him! Can you go find him for me and tell him please, please, please do not get on that plane?"

"No." He turns his back to me.

I circle to the front of him so we are facing each other again. "*No?*"

"No." He turns again and starts to walk away.

What is it with everyone telling me no today?

"Please, Gus! I'm begging you! His flight is about to take off in ten minutes. If you could just go look for me…"

"I'm working. I'm not an errand boy."

I grab my wallet out of my purse, desperate. "What if I gave you $50, would you go look for me then?" I raise my eyebrows and give him a hopeful smile.

"Ma'am, I don't know you, and I'm gonna be honest. I don't like you. I think you're nuts. I can't help you with this. Good luck and Happy Holidays."

And with that, he walks away, leaving me standing there without hope.

"CAN I get a glass of pinot noir, please?"

I am back at the bar in the airport where we had our first drink together.

The bartender drops off my wine and I take a sip. It hits the same as it did that first night. It's terrible and makes my mouth pucker.

I drink it anyway. I deserve bad wine.

Dejected, I play with the mistletoe Doris gave me at the inn.

Callie - 0 Evil Mistletoe - 2

I should have known carrying it with me would curse me.

I ruined everything. I found a wonderful man who supported me, and was willing to give up his own dream so I could be happy, and I ruined it all.

None of the rest of it matters without Gabe.

I'm taking another sip of the awful wine that makes my body shake when I hear him.

"Can you believe someone once told me that mistletoe is evil?"

I turn to see Gabe standing behind me, luggage by his side, smiling. My eyes well up with tears as I rise to stand.

"Why would anyone ever say something so ridiculous?" I say, my voice cracking with emotion.

"I think she sometimes assumes the worst to protect herself from pain. It can be easier to find faults than it is to trust."

"Sounds like she's pretty messed up. You should probably run for the hills and cut your losses."

"It's all just a defense mechanism. I'll have to introduce you to her sometime. She's talented, strong, caring, and brilliant. Security guards hate her, even if they tend to do her bidding."

I smile and wrap both of my arms around him. "Grumpy Gus for the win! I knew I liked that guy."

He reaches for the mistletoe I left on the bar and dangles it over our heads, wrapping his other arm around my waist.

"The last time we were here you said something bad happened every time you were around mistletoe. Care to reverse the curse?"

I look into his eyes and have never felt so blessed and loved. He leans down, and as he is about to kiss me, he whispers, "I love you, Callie."

My heart soars, warmth filling my chest. He still loves me.

"I love you, too."

We kiss, and in that moment, all of my fears melt away.

EPILOGUE

GABE

"Watch it with that thing!"

Callie wielding a sledgehammer is a sight to be seen. She proudly swings it high up on her shoulder and it is so heavy she loses her balance, almost tipping over, laughing.

There is something incredible about a woman who can wear a pair of stained, ripped jeans, a flannel, and safety goggles, and still be the most gorgeous woman in the room.

Callie's voice echoes throughout the empty space. "Gabe, this is it! We're finally doing this. You sure you don't want to grab one too and knock some of this wall down with me?"

"Baby, it's all you." She is beaming like a little kid on Christmas morning. "Make all our dreams come true."

She grins at me, sheer joy emanating from her eyes. She has worked so hard for this moment. J&M will officially start the renovation of the building tomorrow morning, but she insisted on being the one to bust through the first wall. She wanted to jump right in with a hammer the minute it was official. Thankfully, I was able to convince her to wait until we could have Mike mark which wall was safe.

Needless to say, she is raring to get started.

She takes a deep breath, winds up, and slams the sledge-hammer into the wall, over and over, until she can see through to the other side.

"Wow, if that wasn't the sexiest thing I've ever seen." I walk over and wrap my arms around her. "How did it feel?"

"Amazing. I can't believe this is all happening. Do you realize we are standing where the new wine tasting bar will be?"

"How convenient because I brought this." I walk over and grab a bag which contains a bottle of wine from my family's vineyard and two wineglasses. "I think we should be the first to toast here and celebrate this new adventure."

I pour two glasses, and we settle onto the floor, all smiles.

"To Honey's!" I say. We clank our glasses together and take a sip.

Callie is looking around, joyfully dazed, and then turns to me, suddenly serious.

"Gabe."

"Yes, Callie." I say in mock seriousness to match her tone.

"You make me better."

My face softens and everything inside me explodes. "What makes you say that?"

"You challenge me. You support me. You lift me up in ways I didn't even know I needed. When I doubt myself or fear the worst, you show me another way to be. You make me better." Her eyes fill, and she smiles softly, reaching out to grab my hand. "I love you, Gabe."

"I love you, too." I put my glass down and lean in, kissing her passionately. "But you know this is only just the beginning for us, right? Together, we can do anything. I hope you're up for the ride."

ACKNOWLEDGMENTS

Writing this novel with three crazy littles at home in the midst of a global pandemic could not have been possible without the unending support of my incredible husband, Tim. You are my biggest fan and my calm in the storm. Thank you for always lifting me up when I feel like I am about to fall. You are my happily ever after and the one who makes me realize all things are possible.

To my sisters, Farrah and Shannon, the 2 and 4, of 2, 3, 4. I could never have written this without you holding my hand. Thank you for being my ultimate romance guru's and for all the laughs along the way.

Dick and Diane, I am so blessed to have you in my life. Thank you for always being there and for giving me the gift of time.

Thank you to all who support me in J14, and especially to Amanda and Shannah for your honesty and beta reading for me!

Stephanie at Alt 19 Creative, thank you for this gorgeous cover! You were a dream to collaborate with and I can't wait to work with you again.

Thank you to my sweet pup Lucy for looking adorable by my side while I'm writing and giving me much needed snuggle breaks.

God, thank you for granting me the courage to put pen to paper and finally make my dream a reality.

And most of all, thank you, dear reader, for picking up this book and going on this journey with me. I am eternally grateful.

Evelyn Mae is obsessed with swoon worthy romance novels. An ivy league graduate and former high school English teacher, she firmly believes in the power of a good cup of coffee, all things chocolate, and positive thinking.

Evelyn is living out her own happily ever after in Connecticut with her endlessly supportive husband, three spunky daughters, and wimpy, yet lovable, dog, Lucy. When she is not writing or binge reading, she enjoys collecting memes, pretending to have her life together, and trying not to hurt herself doing yoga.